LARRY DEXTER AND THE BANK MYSTERY

LARRY DEXTER
AND THE
BANK MYSTERY
OR, EXCITING DAYS IN WALL STREET

RAYMOND SPERRY

WILDSIDE PRESS

Originally published in 1912.
Published by Wildside Press LLC.
Visit us online at wildsidepress.com.

PREFACE

My Dear Boys:

It is some time since I wrote for you the previous stories about Larry Dexter, and how the young reporter made his successful search for the millionaire. Now I have the privilege of once more relating to you some of his doings.

You know that a reporter's life is full of surprises. One day he may be at a ball game, and the next he may be sent to "cover" a war in China, or to get a story of the work on the Panama Canal.

It was this way with Larry Dexter. One morning he came to the office, after having had some trouble in the subway with a young man, to find his city editor waiting for him with an assignment to solve a million-dollar bank robbery.

Needless to say, Larry at once "got busy." He managed to get the story of the big theft, and then he went on the trail of the man he thought had the money. How he traced him, how he worked up the various clews, his troubles, his disappointments, and the big surprise that awaited him—all this you will find told of in this book.

I hope you will like the story as well as you have the other ones I have written for you, and I trust that you will be glad to hear more of Larry Dexter in another book to follow this one.

Yours very truly,
Raymond Sperry.

CHAPTER I
A BIG ROBBERY

"ONE side there! Get out the way! Do you want to block up the whole entrance? I'm in a hurry!"

"I beg your pardon," began Larry Dexter, "I didn't mean to—"

He had no time to finish the sentence, for the man who had thus rudely spoken brushed against Larry, almost hurling him from his feet, and now fairly ran down the steps leading to the subway station.

"Say, if I'd have known he was going to act that way about it, I'd never have started to ask his pardon," murmured the young reporter, as he rubbed his shoulder, which had hit against the side wall with considerable force.

"He sure was in a hurry, Mr. Dexter," observed the newsboy, who had a small stand at the subway entrance. "Any one would think there was only one train downtown this morning, and if he missed that he couldn't get another."

"That's right, Jim," agreed Larry, as he tossed a coin to the boy of whom, every morning, he purchased several papers, that he might look them over on his trip downtown. For Larry was fast becoming known as the "star" reporter on the New York *Leader*, an afternoon journal. And, as he had to begin his duties in the morning, he always liked to see what the news of the day was likely to be, by scanning some rival sheets.

"Some folks want more than their share, anyhow," went on the newsboy. "I see lots of 'em here. Say, but that was a big fire last night, Mr. Dexter. It ain't out yet."

"So I see," remarked the young reporter, for he and Jim had grown to be quite friendly during the year or more that Larry had been buying papers at this stand. "I expect we'll have to get a story on it ourselves. There may be some new ends to cover. Well, I guess I've given that fellow who was in a hurry plenty of time to get a train ahead of me. I don't want to meet him again," and with that, nodding a friendly good-bye to the newsboy, Larry started down the subway steps.

He was wondering what sort of an assignment might be given him to "cover," or work on, that day, as he bought his ticket and dropped it into the chopper's box. As he strolled out on the platform, built under the sidewalk, and along which the subway express would soon rumble, Larry looked up and down the long stretch of underground pavement.

"Guess I missed the express," he mused. "It was that fellow's fault, too."

He glanced over the headings of the several papers he had purchased, and noted that a story he had written the day before for his own publication, had been used in a number of the rival sheets. This is always a gratification to a reporter.

"Guess they found I hadn't missed much on that yarn," said Larry to himself. "I was up against some hard work, too. Pshaw, I wish I hadn't missed that express. I'll be late if I wait for the next one, and if I take a local, that stops at all the stations, I'll be worse off than ever. I'd like to see that fellow, and give him a bit of my mind. If he hadn't been in such a hurry to get past me, we could have both made the express."

Almost as Larry formed this thought he looked down the platform again, and, to his surprise, he saw the same young man step from behind a big iron pillar. He was eagerly looking over a paper, and did not seem to notice our hero.

"Humph!" mused Larry. "He didn't get the express, after all. He had his trouble for his pains. I'm glad of it. He's a regular bully, I guess," and the young reporter looked closely at the individual who had caused the trouble. True, Larry might have been a bit at fault himself, for he had stood in the subway entrance as he was buying his papers, though, as he thought of it afterward, he knew there was plenty of room for the bully to have passed.

The fellow on whom Larry's eyes were fixed was about the young reporter's own age. He was well dressed, but there was a nervous, hurried manner in all his movements, and two or three times he looked up from the paper he held, glancing about the platform, as though he feared he might see some one whom he did not want to encounter.

All at once his eyes fell upon Larry, and he started visibly. Then he stepped back behind the pillar, as though to hide.

"Guess he thought I might try to make trouble for him," mused Larry. "Well, he deserves it, but I'm not fond of rows, though he did give my shoulder a hard bang. It'll be black and blue, I guess."

The platform was beginning to be thronged with persons now, for the passengers who had accumulated just before Larry arrived had been whirled on their way downtown, and now a second crowd was on hand. This would be repeated several times, until the busy workers had all been transported to their stores or offices.

"I wonder what his object could have been, to rush down here, in plenty of time to have taken the express, and then wait?" thought Larry. "He's a queer one."

"City Hall Express!" suddenly called one of the subway guards, as the distant rumble of a train was heard. "Fourteenth street the first stop! City Hall Express!"

Larry lived well uptown in New York, and it meant a big saving in time to go on an express, that made few stops until City Hall was reached. The office of the *Leader*, where Larry worked, was but a short distance away from the municipal building.

The passengers crowded toward the edge of the platform, in readiness to board the train, the lights of which could now be seen. Larry noticed that the "pusher," as he mentally called him, was standing not far away.

"If he runs into me again," thought the young reporter, "I'll be tempted to punch him, and take what follows. He ought to be taught a lesson."

There was quite a throng about Larry, including a number of young ladies, as the train pulled in, and stopped with a grinding and screeching of brakes. The passengers crowded toward the open doors of the cars.

There was a sudden rush, and Larry noted, with an anger that he could hardly hold back, that the "pusher" was elbowing his way through the press, without any regard for the rights of others. The fellow was just ahead of Larry.

A moment later there was a cry of pain—a girl's cry—and a voice exclaimed:

"Oh! My ankle! You've stepped on it. Oh, dear!"

The young reporter saw a girl, just in front of him, stagger, and almost fall. Larry put out his arm and caught her. At the same time he saw that it was the chap who had previously collided with him who had stepped on the girl's foot, with cruel force.

"What's the matter with you?" demanded Larry, with righteous anger in his voice. "Can't you get on a train without walking all over everybody? Now you take your time!"

Supporting the girl with his left arm, Larry shot out his right hand, caught the fellow by the shoulder, and whirled him about with considerable force. There was sufficient room on the wide platform of the car for Larry to pull the bully back, and, several passengers, seeing what the young reporter was going to do, moved to one side to give him space.

A moment later Larry had fairly shoved the fellow from the car to the station platform.

"Now you can wait until the rest of us get on!" said the young reporter. "And if this young lady wants to make a charge against you, I'll be a witness."

"Say, what's the matter with you, anyhow?" demanded the bully angrily. "I'll punch you good for this!"

"No, you won't," interposed the burly guard of the train. "You didn't get half you deserved. I saw you crowd on, shovin' everybody to one side, and I saw you elbow this young lady. You didn't get more than was comin' to you."

"That's right!" exclaimed several men.

"Unmannerly boor!" said an elderly woman. "If he was down South he'd be taught a lesson!"

"I think he has received the beginning of one now, madam," said an old gentleman, courteously bowing to her.

"All aboard!" sung out the guard, as a warning bell came to him from the car behind, telling him that the doors were closed. "All aboard."

"Can you walk?" asked Larry of the young lady, though, as he looked at her pretty face, he made up his mind that helping her along would not be unpleasant.

"Oh, yes, I'm all right now," she answered with a blush, as she moved on, and away from Larry's supporting arm. "He kicked me in the ankle, and for a moment I couldn't stand. I'm all right now, thank you," and she went into the car with a slight limp.

"You deserve a medal of thanks, young man," said an elderly gentleman to Larry. "That sort of thing is getting all too common in the subway. That fellow ought to ride in a cattle car."

"Well, he isn't going to ride in this one to-day, that's sure," spoke another man, for at that moment, and just as the unmannerly fellow started to get back on board, the guard let the door shut in his face, and the train began to pull out of the station. "He's left, and it serves him right," went on the man with a chuckle, as he glanced at Larry.

"It's the second express he's missed this morning," spoke the young reporter. "He made me miss one, too," and he told of the incident at the head of the subway stairs. As the express rushed on through the tunnel-like blackness, Larry and the men about him entered into an informal conversation about crowds in the subway, and the actions of certain men who seemed to have no regard for the rights of others.

Soon Fourteenth street was reached, and Larry, looking through the car, saw the girl, whom he had assisted, getting ready to go out.

"Guess she works in some of the stores around here," mused the young reporter. "She's pretty all right," and as the girl passed him, on her way to the door, she nodded and smiled brightly. Larry raised his hat, and found himself wishing he knew who she was. He almost made up his mind to take that same express the next morning, on the chance of seeing her again.

"But I hope I don't meet that pushing chap," Larry went on, "for he and I would surely get into a row."

The train rushed on along again, and, a little later, Larry was in the elevator, being lifted to the editorial rooms of the *Leader*, to begin his day's work. He was a little late and he did not like that, for he was generally prompt.

"Hello Larry!" a number of reporters in the local, or city, room greeted our hero as he entered.

"Hello!" he answered back, and, as he was passing on to his desk, one of the copy boys said to him:

"Mr. Emberg wants to see you, Mr. Dexter. He's been asking two or three times if you'd come in yet."

"That's what comes of being late, I suppose," mused our hero as he started for the little room, off the main city one, where Mr. Emberg, city editor of the *Leader*, had his desk and chair.

"Good-morning, Larry," said Mr. Emberg briskly. "I've been waiting for you."

"I'm sorry I was late," answered the reporter. "I started out in time, but I had a couple of experiences with a 'subway porker.' A fellow shoved himself all over. Stepped on a girl's ankle, and there came near being a row. It's funny how selfish some chaps are. Maybe it would make a good story to write something about our overcrowded conditions in the subway."

"Well, maybe," admitted the city editor. "But some one else besides you will have to do it. Never mind about subways, crowds, porkers, or girls who get stepped on this morning, Larry. I've got another assignment for you."

"What is it?"

"Something big. In fact, it's the biggest thing I've put you on since your hunt for the missing millionaire. There's nothing hanging over for you to clean up; is there?"

"No, I'm all through with that church-meeting story."

"Good! Then I want you to get right out after this. It's the biggest thing that's been pulled off in New York in a long time. But it isn't going to be easy to get."

"What is it, Mr. Emberg?"

"Shut the door, Larry, and come over here. I don't want this to get out, for we may pull off a 'scoop' on it."

The young reporter closed the door of the private office, and came closer to the city editor's desk. He knew something unusual must be in prospect when Mr. Emberg was so careful.

"Larry," began the city editor, "there's been a big robbery committed, and the bank that lost the money is trying to keep it quiet for a while, in the hope of tracing the thieves. But I have a private tip about it, and now I want you to get right out on the story, and get it."

"What bank was robbed, Mr. Emberg?"

"The Consolidated National. Some time in the past week one million dollars in currency was stolen, and they can't get a trace of it, or the thief, or thieves, who got away with it. It's the biggest bank mystery that's happened in years, and if you possibly can, Larry, I want you to get a scoop out

9

of it. I don't believe any other papers know about it yet, and if you go at it right you can make a big story."

"A million dollars stolen!" gasped Larry. "I should say it was a big robbery."

"A corker!" exclaimed Mr. Emberg admiringly, not because of the criminal action, however, so much as for the chance of a big story for his paper. "A corker, Larry. Get right after it, and, if you can find the money, or the thieves—well, that will make it all the better. Get busy!"

"I will," answered the reporter, as he hurried out of the room. And Larry had started on an assignment that was to lead him to the solution of one of the strangest mysteries ever known, and destined to further add to his laurels as a "star" reporter.

"Go at it in your own way, Larry," the city editor called after him. "There's no limit to your expense bills. Just get the story and beat all the other papers."

"I will!" answered Larry again.

CHAPTER II
TURNED DOWN

WHILE Larry Dexter is on his way to the Consolidated National Bank, to use his wits in order to get the story of the robbery, which it seemed that the bank officials did not want made public as yet, I will take a few moments to tell my new readers something of the youth who is to be the hero of this book.

Many of you have met Larry before. I first introduced him to you in the initial volume of this series, entitled, "Larry Dexter at the Big Flood," and in that I told how Larry, with his mother, his sisters Lucy and Mary, and his brother James, had come to New York, after the death of Mr. Dexter, and the selling of the old farm.

Larry had always had an ambition to become a reporter on a big metropolitan paper, and, after hard work, he succeeded. He began as a boy who carried copy, or the articles which the reporters write for the paper, from the editors' desks to the tubes where it was shot to the composing room, where the printers set it up.

Larry soon proved that he had a "nose for news," and he was made a reporter. From then on his rise was rapid. In the second book, called "Larry Dexter and the Land Swindlers," I related some of the adventures in the great city, and how he got on the trail of a band of unscrupulous men, and foiled their plans.

Larry soon had almost developed into what is called a "star" reporter. That is, one to whom comes the honor of working up the big stories of the day. Instead of covering routine work he would be given difficult tasks to do, and special articles to write, for that is the test of a good reporter.

One of the most difficult tasks to which Larry was ever assigned was to find a certain rich man who had disappeared. In the third volume of the series, called "Larry Dexter and the Missing Millionaire," I gave the details of his hunt for the missing millionaire.

Mr. Hampton Potter, the millionaire, was one day reported as missing. It seemed a complete mystery, but Larry found out all about, and even located Mr. Potter himself. The millionaire had disappeared for business reasons, and in order to perfect certain deals involving large sums, and, though at first his wife, and his daughter Grace, were much worried, they finally received a note from Mr. Potter, stating that he was safe.

11

But this only served to make matters more complicated, and Larry was more baffled than ever. During the time the young reporter worked on the case he became quite well acquainted with Miss Grace Potter, who was an exceedingly pretty girl. Finally, as I have said, Mr. Potter was located, and his enemies, who sought to do him harm, were vanquished. Of course Larry got an exclusive story out of it, in addition to rendering the Potter family a big service.

"But I guess I'm going to have my own troubles on this bank mystery robbery," mused Larry, as he journeyed toward the financial institution, which was one of the largest in New York city. "If they're keeping it quiet, that means there's something back of it, and the officials won't want to give out the story. But I've got to get it, somehow.

"Let's see, do I know anybody in the Consolidated National?" and Larry went hastily over his rather lengthy list of acquaintances. For it is through friends and acquaintances that a reporter often gets his best news. "No, I can't recall anybody down there," Larry went on. "Hold on, though —why, yes! That's the very thing! Mr. Hampton Potter is one of the biggest depositors there. His name ought to have some weight. If I can't get at the president, or cashier, in any other way, Mr. Potter may help me. If the bank has been looted, he'll know about it as soon as anybody.

"I hope they haven't got any of his wealth, though," and Larry had a memory of a certain pretty girl to whom wealth meant much, as she had been used to it all her life. "It would go hard with Grace Potter to be poor," thought the reporter, "though I'm sure she'd make the best of it, if it had to be. That's what I'll do. If the bank people won't give me the story, I'll see Mr. Potter," and with this thought completed Larry found himself in front of the looted bank in Wall street.

"There doesn't seem to be much excitement going on," mused the reporter as he mounted the bank steps, and noted that everything inside the institution seemed to be as quiet as is ordinarily the case in moneyed institutions. Depositors were coming and going as if nothing had happened, the discount clerks, the bookkeepers, cashiers and tellers were in their regular places, carrying on the business of the bank. And yet Larry's trained observation told him that there was a certain strained atmosphere over it all.

Not on the part of the depositors. They seemed to know nothing about it. But the clerks, cashiers, tellers, and, in fact, all the employees, seemed to be under some nervous strain. It was as if they expected an explosion at any moment.

"I'd like to see Mr. Wesley Bentfield," said Larry to a uniformed porter, or messenger, in the open corridor of the institution. Mr. Bentfield was the bank's president, and Larry decided that it was best to go to the chief officer at once, and not waste time on subordinates.

"The president is very busy," replied the messenger, with a quick glance at Larry. "I don't believe he'll see you."

"Just take my card in," suggested the reporter, handing over a bit of pasteboard with his own name and that of the *Leader* on it. "Tell him it's very important."

The uniformed messenger was soon back, and he looked at Larry with increased respect.

"Mr. Bentfield will see you, sir," he said.

"I thought he would," remarked Larry grimly. More than one closed door has been opened by the magic of a newspaper reporter's card. Larry followed the messenger to the president's private room. The reporter found the head of the bank, and several other gentlemen, seated in front of a large table.

One glance was enough to tell Larry that something had occurred— something serious, to judge by the worried faces of the financiers. The youth decided to come to the point at once. Looking boldly at Mr. Bentfield, whom he recognized from having noted his portrait in the papers many times, Larry said:

"I have information, Mr. Bentfield, that your bank has lost a large sum of money."

"Lost? How?" asked the president, as if in surprise.

"By robbery!"

"Who told you?" interposed one of the other men.

"I am not at liberty to say," replied Larry, for Mr. Emberg, in giving him the source of the "tip," had cautioned him to say nothing about it. In fact, a private detective agency, to which the bank had appealed, had informed, or "tipped off," the city editor. As this was not supposed to be done, naturally the detective who gave the "tip" wanted to be protected, and a newspaper man always holds inviolate, if so requested, the source of his information.

"I'm afraid I have no news for you," spoke the president calmly, yet Larry noted a nervous twitching of Mr. Bentfield's hands.

"You mean you *won't* tell me," suggested Larry with a smile. He had met such obstinacy before.

"We have nothing for the press," said Mr. Bentfield firmly.

"Then I shall have to get my information elsewhere, I suppose," went on Larry calmly. "I might say that I know that this bank has lost a million dollars—"

"Hush!" exclaimed one of the directors in a startled whisper. "You'll start a panic!"

"How can I, if there has been no robbery?" asked Larry quickly.

"Well, er—even the *rumor* of a robbery might do it, and cause a run on the bank," lamely explained the man who had begged Larry to keep quiet.

"I should be sorry to do that," spoke the young reporter firmly, "but I am after this story, and I'm going to get it. If not from here, then from somewhere else. I would rather have you tell me," he said, looking at the president, "as then the facts would be more complete and accurate. But I am going to get the story, anyhow. I know your bank has lost a million, and, sooner or later, the facts will come out. Why don't you tell me?" he asked of Mr. Bentfield.

"I have no information for the press," said the president coldly. "I believe that is all I can say to you. And I think my associates will agree with me."

He looked around at the other men, all of whom nodded their heads gravely. Larry felt that he was "up against it," as he had feared would be the case. But he was not done yet.

"Is that your last word?" he asked. "Remember the *Leader* has reliable information on this story, and remember, also, that it is bound to come out. It might better be given straight than to have it pieced out more or less inaccurately."

"If you've got the story, why don't you print it?" challenged a little man with a black moustache. "But I warn you, that if you make trouble for this bank your paper shall answer for it!"

"We don't want to make trouble," said Larry with a confident smile, "but we want the story, and we're going to get it! We'll take our medicine, too."

"Impudent reporters!" muttered another director, and Larry smiled. He was used to this sort of treatment, and was, by this time, hardened to it.

"There is nothing further for you," again said the president coldly. "And, as we are having a directors' meeting, I shall have to ask you to leave, Mr. er—Mr. Leader."

"Dexter, if you please," corrected Larry with a smile. "Well, you may read the story in this afternoon's paper," he said boldly, as he left.

"Upstart!" snapped the man with the black moustache. "The papers ought to be suppressed."

Larry was doing some hard thinking as he went out. He had been turned down at his first trial, but that had often been the case before, and it only made him all the more resolved to get the story at any cost.

"I'll see what Mr. Potter can do for me," he mused as he hurried down the steps of the bank. As he did so he saw a young man approaching the building in a hurry.

"Peter Manton, of the *Scorcher*!" exclaimed Larry, as he recognized his former enemy. "He's after the story too! I wonder if I can scoop him? I hope he doesn't see me."

14

Larry dodged behind an automobile that stood at the curb, and was successful in getting away as Peter ran up the bank steps.

"The trail is getting hot," thought Larry. "Other papers have tips about the robbery! I've just *got* to get that scoop!"

CHAPTER III
LARRY GETS THE SCOOP

THE office of Mr. Hampton Potter, the millionaire, was not far from the bank where Harry had tried unsuccessfully to get the story of the robbery. The young reporter was soon in front of the big structure where Mr. Potter had rooms, and he sent in his card.

"Show Mr. Dexter in at once," commanded the wealthy man, when he had read our hero's name. "I wonder if he thinks I'm missing again," mused Mr. Potter with a laugh, as he awaited Larry's arrival. "More than likely, though, that he wants a story about the stock market," for, several times since Larry had helped Mr. Potter get the best of his enemies, the two had met, and Larry often picked up a choice and exclusive bit of news from his rich friend.

"Well, what is it going to be to-day, Larry?" asked Mr. Potter, as the young reporter entered. "Do you want something about the bulls and the bears playing havoc with the market?"

"It's something more important than that, Mr. Potter."

"More important?" Something in the reporter's face made the millionaire guess that the lad was on the trail of a big story. "What is it, Larry?"

Our hero came close to the desk of his rich friend, and, in a voice that was almost a whisper, he said:

"Mr. Potter, the Consolidated National Bank has been robbed of a million dollars. They are keeping the matter quiet, though a private detective agency is working on the case. I went there and asked for the story. I was turned down, and so I come to you. You're a big depositor there, aren't you?"

"I am, Larry. But, Great Scott! A robbery of a million! You must be mistaken. Such a thing could not happen. A million dollars!"

"That's right," said the lad. "I got it from my city editor, on good authority. Now look here, Mr. Potter, I want that story. I want to get it exclusively. The bank people know the facts, but they won't talk. If they've lost a million it's the right of the public to know it. Maybe the depositors unknowingly are keeping on putting money in a bank which is on the verge of failure. It isn't right! The story ought to come out. You're a big depositor. If you go to the president and demand the facts he'll have to tell them to you. Then you can tell me, and I'll have my scoop. See?"

"I do, Larry. But, Great Scott! A million gone! And they're keeping it quiet! Why, I made a big deposit there, only yesterday!"

He thought deeply for a moment, and Larry watched him closely. Would the millionaire aid him to get the story?

"A million gone!" said Mr. Potter, half to himself. "I had a right to know that, and, by Jove, I *will* know it. I'll call up Bentfield, and demand to know why he's keeping this quiet. I'll get him on the wire!"

He reached for the telephone.

"Don't do that!" cried Larry quickly.

"Why not?"

"Because there'll be a leak in the central office, or some one will overhear it, and then the story will be out. I don't want it to get loose until it comes out in the *Leader*. I want it all alone. There's another reporter after it —Peter Manton—with whom I had a lot of trouble when I first came to New York, though we're friendly enough now. But, for all that, I want to beat him on this story, if I can. He quit the newspaper game for a while and went into real estate. Now he's reporting again. I want to beat him."

"Oh, I suppose so," agreed Mr. Potter. "I see what you mean, Larry. Well, I'll not telephone. I'll go see Bentfield personally. You stay here, and as soon as I have the facts I'll come back and tell you. I haven't forgotten what you did for me. How soon must you have the story?"

"Oh, if I get it by twelve o'clock I can 'phone it, and catch the first main edition. I'd like to hold it for the last, and then the other papers couldn't use it until late to-night, or to-morrow morning, but I'm afraid it won't keep. It's too big."

"I guess you're right," agreed Mr. Potter. "Well, I'll get it for you as soon as I can," and, calling his secretary, he gave the man certain instructions, also arranging to have Larry wait in the private office until his return.

"I'll be as quick as I can," remarked the millionaire, with a smile, as he started out. "I'm a sort of special reporter now; eh, Larry?"

"Something like that, Mr. Potter. Please don't 'fall down.'"

"Eh? What's that? Is it slippery out?" and, somewhat surprised, he looked from his window into the pleasant spring sunshine.

"No, I meant don't 'fall down' on the assignment—don't miss getting it."

"Oh, I see! Well, I'll do my best," and he laughed.

It seemed a long time for Larry to wait until the millionaire returned, and the young reporter kept looking at his watch as if that would hasten matters. Afterward Larry learned that Mr. Potter had even engaged a taxicab in order to come and go more quickly, for he felt a real liking for our hero, and wanted to help him.

Mr. Potter re-entered his office. There was a look on his face that told Larry he had been successful, and had secured the story.

"Well?" asked the reporter anxiously.

"It's true!" exclaimed the millionaire. "I would never have believed it possible that a million dollars could have been stolen so easily. But it's gone! It's a great mystery."

"Did they hesitate about telling you?" asked Larry.

"They did, until I demanded to know, as my right, and I threatened to inform the banking commissioner if they did not let me know all the facts. They wanted to know where I got my information, but I didn't tell. The bank is solvent, however, though the loss is a heavy one. The depositors will lose nothing. Now here are the facts, as far as they're known, and that isn't much. It's a queer mystery."

"A mystery; how?" asked Larry.

"Why, the way the money disappeared. It was almost like magic. I'll tell you the main facts, and you can elaborate on them later.

"It happened three days ago, and they've been keeping it quiet since— aside from the detectives knowing it—in the hopes that the thieves could be traced. But so far nothing has come of it. Now here's the story."

And as Mr. Potter told it, Larry rapidly made notes so he could write the account for his paper.

It seemed that at eleven o'clock, one morning, four tellers of the Con-solidated National Bank counted out from the vault one million dollars in thousand-dollar bills. The money was made up into ten packages of one hundred thousand dollars each, carefully checked over by the chief cashier, and then this immense sum was placed in a large leather bag, to be taken to the vaults of the Metropolitan National Bank. It was to be used in a govern-ment bond transaction the following day.

The valise into which the money was placed was lined with steel wire, for sometimes bold thieves attack bank messengers in New York's financial district, slit open, with keen knives, the bags they carry, and get the bundles of bills. It was to prevent any such theft as this that a steel-mesh-lined bag was used.

The Metropolitan Bank was to send a messenger to get the money from the Consolidated Bank at noon, and, pending the arrival of this man, the bag, containing the million dollars, was placed on the floor in the Consoli-dated Bank, close to the chief cashier's desk.

"Then this is what happened next," said Mr. Potter, after telling the story thus far.

"Luke Tucker, the messenger from the bank that was to receive the large sum in bills, arrived promptly on time. To assist him in carrying the bag William French, a messenger from the Consolidated Bank, was as-

18

signed. To the keeping of these two men the bag was entrusted, and the handle of it was handcuffed to the left wrist of French, so that if a bold thief tried to grab it he would have to take the man along too.

"Adam Force, a special officer from the Consolidated Bank, walked out after the two messengers who, between them, carried the bag holding a million dollars," continued Mr. Potter, while Larry went on making notes. "Force is a very trustworthy man. He used to work for me. In his coat pocket, as he strolled along behind the messengers, he held a loaded revolver, ready for instant use should a robbery be attempted.

"From the Consolidated Bank to the Metropolitan it is less than half a mile, and absolutely nothing happened on the way. The messengers and the detective arrived safely with the bag, and it was unlocked from the handcuff on the wrist of French. A receipt was to be given for the money, but, before this was done, as is always the case, four tellers of the receiving bank proceeded to check over the bundles of bills.

"The bag was opened, Larry, in the presence of half a dozen men, but, instead of seeing the neat bundles of bank bills, there were only some bricks, wrapped in newspapers, in the valise."

"Bricks!" cried Larry, all excitement.

"Bricks," answered Mr. Potter grimly.

"But where had the money gone?" asked the reporter. "If no one attacked them on the trip, if the money was in the valise when it left the first bank—how could it have been taken?"

"That's the mystery," replied Mr. Potter. "No one seems to know how the money got out. It was utterly impossible for it to have disappeared after the bag was locked on French's wrist. Every one agrees on that point."

"Then it was done before the valise left the Consolidated Bank," decided Larry promptly.

"That's my opinion," decided the millionaire. "But how was it done? The four tellers stood by, and saw the million dollars put in. Then the valise was double locked, and set down by the chief cashier's desk. He says he was there all the while, and yet, when the other bank's tellers open the satchel, they find bricks instead of money. That's the mystery. It's like a conjurer's trick. And that's your story, Larry."

"And a mighty big story it is, too!" cried the young reporter "I'm ever so much obliged to you, Mr. Potter. I think I've got the biggest scoop of years. I'm going to make a good story of it, and play up that mystery for all it's worth. May I use your telephone?"

"Yes—but, for the same reason that you cautioned me, I wouldn't 'phone the story in if I were you. It might get out."

"Oh, I'm not going to tell the story over the wire," spoke Larry. "I just want to let Mr. Emberg know I've got it."

And, in a few seconds, he was talking to his city editor.

"That's it, Larry! That's fine! Great!" fairly shouted Mr. Emberg. "Get right in with the yarn! We'll hold the whole first page for you if you need it. Rush!"

Larry hung up the telephone receiver, glanced over his notes to see if there were any details on which he wanted to ask questions, and then started from the millionaire's office.

"There's a taxicab outside," said Mr. Potter. "I told the man to wait, thinking you'd like to use it to get back to your office in a hurry."

"Thanks," spoke Larry. "I'll take it."

"And come up and see us soon," requested the millionaire. "Grace was asking for you the other day. Don't wait to solve this bank mystery, but come any time."

"I will," promised the young reporter, and then, fairly jumping into the elevator, he shot downward and hurled himself into the waiting taxi.

"The *Leader* office as fast as you can make it!" cried Larry, and the auto swung up Wall street, toward Broadway, at a fast rate of speed. As Larry passed the robbed bank he looked out. He saw his rival, Peter Manton, coming down the steps, and there was a look on his face that seemed to show defeat.

"I don't believe he got the yarn," chuckled our hero. "I think I can scoop him!"

Larry fairly rushed into the office of his paper and flew to the city room.

"Got it all?" asked Mr. Emberg, coming out of his room.

"All about the robbery. The mystery is yet to be solved," answered Larry breathlessly.

"Good! We can string it along for a week, maybe!" said the editor gleefully. "Pound it out for all you're worth. Here, boy, go down to the 'morgue' and get me out pictures of the Consolidated Bank and all the officials. We'll spread on this!"

Larry was soon at his typewriter, clicking off the big story—the biggest story of the day. In order to catch the first extra edition, Mr. Emberg handled Larry's copy himself, taking it page by page as it came from the machine.

It was rushed up to the composing room through the pneumatic tubes, and there it was cut into small sections, or "takes," so that several printers could work on it at once.

Rapidly the type-setting machines were putting into solid form Larry's big, million-dollar robbery story. Mr. Emberg wrote a "scare" head for it, and the printers began setting that up. Down in the art department a "layout" of several pictures was being gotten ready, showing the looted bank, and portraits of its officers.

Soon enough of Larry's story for one edition was finished, and he could take his time on the more unimportant details. Meanwhile other reporters had been sent out to get interviews as to the possible effect on the financial market by the loss of a million dollars from one bank. Some reporters looked up the big robberies of past years, to compare them with the present million-dollar one.

Then the paper came out. The immense presses down in the basement thundered away, fairly showering out the folded copies of the *Leader*, ready for the boys to sell on the street.

"Extra! Extra!" the lads cried, as they sped through the streets. "Extra! Full account of de great bank myst'ry! Million dollars stole! Extra! Extra!"

Larry sat back in his chair for a moment's rest. He was tired from his morning's task, and the pounding of the typewriter keys. But he was happy.

"If only the other papers haven't got the story!" he said to himself. "If I have a scoop! If I have beaten Peter Manton!"

And he had. When the *Leader's* rivals' sheets came out not one of them had the story of the million-dollar bank robbery, and only a few had a hint that anything was wrong, financially, with the institution. Only hints were given.

"That's the best Peter could do," said Larry joyfully, as he looked over the other papers. "He didn't get the story."

"No, you scored a clean beat, Larry," said Mr. Emberg proudly. "It was great work! But it can't stop there."

"What do you mean?"

"I mean that you've got to keep right on with this story. Larry, I'm going to give you the biggest assignment you ever had. I want you to find out where that million dollars went, and who took it. Find the thief, Larry, and get the story of the mystery. It's up to you. From now on you're to do nothing but keep on this bank case. Live in Wall street if you have to. Stay there night and day, but get the story. It's up to you!"

"All right," spoke the young reporter rather solemnly. "I'll do my best."

"Go down to the bank now," suggested Mr. Emberg, "and show them our story. Maybe they'll be willing to talk after they see what we have printed."

CHAPTER IV
LARRY AT THE BANK

THERE was quite a different scene being enacted in the Consolidated National Bank when Larry arrived there, about three o'clock on the afternoon of the day his story of the robbery came out, and proved such a sensational "beat," than there was on his first visit. As the young reporter entered the institution, he saw an excited crowd of men, and some women, in line at the paying teller's window. Inside the brass gratings clerks, cashiers and other employees were very busy.

"It looks like a run," remarked Larry, half to himself, as he stood in the corridor, and watched the crowd of evidently frightened depositors.

"It *is* a run, young man!" exclaimed a nervous tradesman, who had a check in one hand, and a copy of Larry's paper in the other. "I didn't know about the loss, though, until I read this," and he tapped the folded journal nervously.

"A run! I should say so!" exclaimed another man, who also clutched a *Leader*. "A million-dollar robbery! This bank can never stand that loss. It'll fail, and I'm going to get my money out before that happens."

"The same here," added several, who were crowding up to get in line at the paying teller's window.

"A run on the bank," mused Larry. "This will make more news! I must 'phone it in. I'm sorry if my story started this, but I can't help it. The president might have given me the story when I first asked for it, and then he would have had a chance to explain that the bank could stand the loss. This would have given the depositors confidence. But he wouldn't do it."

If there was any doubt in Larry's mind that the story which he had written had caused the run-scare it was soon over, for every person who crowded into the bank carried a copy of the *Leader*, with our hero's big scoop on the front page.

"And there isn't another New York paper to be seen," chuckled Larry. "I've beaten 'em all! Well, now to send word in about the run. They can add that to the general yarn."

He was about to hurry from the bank, his thoughts busy with many things, but chiefly how he might set about his task of discovering the thief, and the missing million, when he saw President Bentfield come hurriedly from his private office.

"I might as well wait and see what's up," thought the young reporter. "I may get another scoop."

There was little chance of this, however, for, on looking about, he saw reporters of several other papers present. Among them was Peter Manton.

"Hello, Pete!" greeted Larry. "Are you after this?"

"Yes, but it's a hot time to get after it," grumbled Peter. "After your paper scooped us! Was it your yarn?"

"It was," said Larry, with justifiable pride.

"I might have known it," went on the *Scorcher's* reporter. "You have us all skinned. How'd you do it?"

"That's telling," replied Larry, with a smile.

"I came here to get the story, after some sort of a tip had come in the office," went on Peter, "but there was nothing doing. Bentfield turned me down."

"Yes, I saw you," admitted Larry. "But what's up now?"

Indeed, it was evident that something unusual was in the wind, for President Bentfield was talking excitedly to the clerks and cashiers back of the brass grill, and the anxious depositors, who wanted to withdraw their money, were looking on curiously.

"Gentlemen, your attention for one moment!" suddenly called the bank president, mounting on a box in order to see and be seen. "I wish to make an announcement. After it is over you are all at liberty to withdraw every dollar of your deposits. The bank will remain open for that purpose all night if necessary. But I wish to state that, in spite of the heavy loss we have sustained, we can meet every cent of our obligations. Every depositor can be paid in full, and we will still be doing business. There is no need of a run. Take your time."

"That's easy to say!" exclaimed a nervous woman.

"And easy to prove!" retorted the president quickly. "If you will appoint a delegation I will have the members of it admitted to our vaults. We have cash enough on hand to pay every depositor in full, and I'll show it to you!"

There, was a murmur of gratified surprise at this, and several who had been crowding into line to get their money became more composed. Still, there were doubtful ones.

Several depositors announced themselves as anxious to look into the vaults. They were escorted there and, on coming back, stated that they had seen several millions in currency, or Government bonds. It developed later that, in anticipation of a possible run, when the million-dollar robbery should become known, the bank had, a few days previous, and directly after the theft, stored a large amount of cash in its vaults.

"Are you satisfied?" demanded the president.

"Yes! Yes!" exclaimed the crowd, and it began to melt away. The run was practically over, and the alarm, that had been caused be reading the story in the *Leader*, was at an end.

President Bentfield looked relieved, and started for his private office. The hard-worked clerks and tellers breathed easier.

"This will make good copy," remarked Peter to Larry. "I'm going to 'phone it in."

"So am I," replied our hero, and the two started out on the run, for it was getting late, and every second counts when a paper is going to press.

As Larry passed a door that led from the main corridor into the president's room, the uniformed messenger by whom, earlier in the day, he had sent in his card, came out.

"The president wants to see you, Mr. Dexter," he said.

"I can't see him now," replied Larry, and there was grim satisfaction in his ability to thus repay, in his own coin, the president's treatment of himself. "I'm in a hurry to telephone."

"He said I was to tell you it was very important for him to see you," went on the messenger. "He saw you when he went out to make the announcement about there being plenty of cash. Mr. Bentfield says it's to your interest to see him."

"But I've got to telephone some news in to my paper," answered Larry, chaffing at the delay. "It's to the bank's interest to have it known that there is no danger of a run. Otherwise you'll have a mob of out-of-town depositors around your doors in the morning. I've got to telephone, and I'll see Mr. Bentfield later."

"There's a telephone in his private office," said the messenger. "I was to tell you that you could use that if you wanted to."

Larry's eyes sparkled. He knew the advantage of getting to a telephone quickly when it was close to last edition time, and down in Wall street, in the congested financial district, at this hour of the day, the wires were overburdened with messages. Larry realized that to go out, and hunt up a public pay station, would take time, and he never hoped for such good luck as the chance to use the president's private wire to send in his news.

"Very well," he said, "I'll see Mr. Bentfield."

He was shown into the bank president's room. He found a number of men there, among them Mr. Potter, who looked at him and smiled.

"That reporter!" fairly growled the black-moustached director as he saw Larry. "What does he want now?"

"I have sent for him," replied Mr. Bentfield. "And I may say that I have changed my opinion of newspaper men in the last few hours. Mr. Dexter, I have something to say to you."

"Would you mind if I telephoned this news in to my paper first?" asked Larry respectfully. "It is very important to me, as this is my profession."

"Go right ahead!" said the president, in more genial tones than he had used when Larry saw him before. "Here is my telephone. I'd be glad to have you make as emphatic as possible the announcement I just made. And, after you have 'phoned that in, I'll add some other news that may give you another 'scoop,' as I believe they are called."

Larry's eyes sparkled at hearing this. News was coming his way fast this day—exclusive news, too.

It did not take long to send over the wire the story of the run, and how quickly and dramatically it had been checked, by the prompt action of the president.

"Hold the wire a minute," said Larry, to the reporter in the office who was taking the story from his dictation. "The president has something else to add."

"It is this," spoke Mr. Bentfield, as Larry turned questioningly toward him. All the directors and other gentlemen in the room had been listening curiously to the manner in which Larry told the story over the wire. "We have decided to offer a reward of twenty thousand dollars for the arrest of the person or persons who got our million dollars," said the president. "You may add that to your story. It may be of interest to the public."

"I should say it would!" exclaimed Larry, and then in quick, crisp words he sent that additional information over the wire.

"They're going to put a scare-head on that," the young reporter stated to the president a moment later, still remaining at the telephone.

"Good! It may attract enough attention so that the general public will be interested in earning the reward," remarked Mr. Bentfield. "It may help to arrest the thief."

"I suppose you mean the reward will be paid if the thief is arrested, and the money recovered," suggested Larry.

"No! The reward will be paid for the apprehension of the thief, whether he has a dollar of the money or not!" cried the president. "We want to make an example of him! It is a heavy loss for the bank, but, unless we find out how the robbery was committed, and get the thief, other banks may suffer likewise. The reward is for the thief, not the money!"

Larry added this bit of news, and then, at the suggestion of Mr. Bentfield, he dictated a statement to the effect that the bank officials had not the slightest clue to the thief, and did not suspect any one.

"Our employees feel the stigma keenly enough as it is," the president said, "and this may help to relieve it."

Larry finished telephoning, and sat back with a sigh of relief. He had done good work that day, and it developed later that he had made a second scoop—that about the big reward being offered. He was well satisfied with his assignment.

"And now," began Mr. Bentfield, at the conclusion of the telephoning, "I would like to ask you a question, Mr. Dexter. Where did you get your information about the robbery?"

"I can't tell you," said Larry promptly. "It would be a violation of confidence, of which no newspaper man can ever be guilty."

"Very well," spoke Mr. Bentfield, and he was not at all unpleasant about it. "I will respect your scruples, though I would like very much to know how you reporters get your news. But, since you have it, perhaps it is all for the best. It would have had to come out sooner or later, and perhaps we should have made a statement sooner. Our directors were divided on the subject."

"I'll tell you how Larry Dexter got the story," quickly exclaimed Mr. Potter. "I gave it to him. I felt that the public had a right to know of this big theft."

The statement created surprise, and some of the directors were rather angry at Mr. Potter. But he was a big depositor, and one whom the bank wished to please, so little was said about it.

"Perhaps, after all, it is for the best," agreed the president. "I'm sure I congratulate you, Mr. Dexter, on the clever story you wrote, and the way in which you handled this mystery. For a mystery it is, and I'm afraid we can never solve it."

"Haven't the detectives been able to get any clews?" asked the young reporter.

"Not a one," replied Mr. Bentfield. "We shall now notify the regular police, and let them work on the case as well as the private agency which we engaged."

"I can tell you who will do a good deal better work on this case than the regular detectives, or the private ones, either," said Mr. Potter, during a pause in the talk.

"Who?" demanded several directors at once.

"Larry Dexter!" exclaimed the millionaire. "He found me, when none of the other reporters, or police, could, and I thought I was pretty well hidden. Maybe he could find this thief."

"And the million dollars!" added the black-moustached man eagerly. "That's too big a sum to lose."

"It certainly is," agreed the president. "I have many times heard it said," he went on, "that reporters are often better at solving crimes than the average detective. Perhaps it would be a good plan to have Mr. Dexter take up this case. Will you do it?" he asked. "I think we really need you. Will you act as a detective for us and try to earn that reward?"

"I'm a newspaper man," said Larry simply, "and, though it is true that we often have to do detective work, I must act for my paper first."

"But you could do that and help the bank, too," suggested Mr. Potter. "Larry, I think this is just the chance for you. If you find the thief, and the million, you will have a big 'beat' for your paper. Why don't you do it?"

"I will!" cried Larry. "In fact, my city editor has assigned me to this case, and I'm to do nothing else. But, of course, with the aid of the bank officials I can work to better advantage."

"Then you shall have it!" exclaimed President Bentfield. "Gentlemen, Larry Dexter is to be given every aid in our power to endeavor to solve this bank mystery! And it's my opinion that, if it isn't solved, the Consolidated National will be the laughing stock of Wall street. Think of having a million taken right from under our noses, and not even a clew as to how it disappeared! Mr. Dexter, get busy, please!" and he smiled at our hero. There had come quite a change over Mr. Bentfield in a few hours, and Larry was the cause of it. The president and his associates looked keenly at the young reporter.

CHAPTER V
THE CLEW OF THE SATCHEL

"WELL, what's the first thing to do, Larry?" asked Mr. Potter, with a smile. He had returned to the bank shortly after giving Larry the details of the robbery. "How are you going at it to solve this mystery?"

"I don't know," answered the young reporter frankly. "There are many ends to be covered. I guess I'll have to ask you a lot of questions," he said to the president. "That's how a reporter gets his news," he continued with a smile.

"Ask as many as you like," replied the head of the bank. "We'll give you all the aid possible."

Larry rapidly thought over the case. He wanted to get all the facts clear in his mind.

Several of the directors, who had business elsewhere, left, as there was nothing more they could do at the bank. The arrangements for meeting the heavy financial loss had been made a day or two previous, as soon as the robbery was discovered, and though the credit of the institution was strained to the utmost, it was seen that it could weather the storm.

"I think I understand pretty well how the money was packed in the valise, and taken to the other bank," began Larry after a pause. "Then, as the robbery did not take place outside of this bank, and did not occur in the other bank, it must have been done here—right in your own institution," he said to the president.

"Impossible!" exclaimed the black-moustached man, whose name it developed was Mr. Kent Wilson. "Impossible!"

"Not at all impossible," replied Mr. Bentfield. "In fact, that is the only way to account for it, Mr. Wilson. The detectives are all agreed on that point."

"And you say you do not suspect any of your employees?" asked Larry.

"Not a one, though of course, as is but natural, a watch is being kept over every one, from the smallest messenger boy, up to—well, I may say ourselves," spoke the president. "It is an unpleasant thing to do, but necessary. But it does not seem possible that any of them, working together, or singly, could have taken that money."

"Would it be possible for an outsider to have entered the cashier's cage, and substituted the bag of bricks for the bag of bills?" the young reporter inquired.

"Of course it is possible," admitted the president, "but highly improbable. The entire part of the bank, where the clerks and tellers work, is, as you have seen, fenced off from the outside part, where the depositors enter, by a heavy brass grating. There is even a grating over the top, and the doors are all self-closing, locking automatically from the inside.

"A clever thief might, of course, manipulate a door, and so enter the cage, but his presence would at once be noticed, and an alarm given. No one, not an employee of the bank, is allowed back of the grating on any pretext whatever. An alarm would be instantly given should such a thing occur. So I don't see how it is possible that an outsider took the money."

"Then it comes right back to the other proposition, that some one connected with the bank did it," decided Larry, "and I think we've got to work on that theory."

"Impossible! Impossible!" exclaimed Mr. Wilson impatiently. "Our employees are all to be trusted."

"It is hard to know what to believe," admitted the president. "Are there any other questions you would like to ask, Mr. Dexter?"

"Several," replied Larry, "but I want to think them over first. Could I borrow the bag in which the bricks instead of money were taken to the other bank?" he requested.

"Borrow the valise?" exclaimed the president. "What for?"

"Because I believe it will prove a valuable clew," was the answer. "It is the start in solving this mystery. Where is the valise?"

"It is here," spoke Mr. Bentfield, and, going to a closet, he took out the satchel which had played such an important part in the big theft.

"Is it exactly the same as the one ordinarily used by your bank, when money is to be carried through the streets?" asked Larry, as he looked at the satchel.

"No, not exactly," replied the president. "The outside, the kind of leather and its general appearance are almost identical. But the lining of steel wire is not in this valise. I suppose the thief did not consider it necessary to provide that in this duplicate satchel, as it could only be seen by tearing out the inner leather lining."

"Then this is point number one," said Larry, making a note of it. "The thief got a valise as nearly like the regular one used as possible."

"There's something in that!" exclaimed Mr. Potter. "Did your regular, or private detectives, think of that, Mr. Bentfield?"

"No, they did not. Mr. Dexter, I am beginning to have hopes that you will yet get to the bottom of this."

"It's too soon to hope yet," replied Larry. "Now, if you will let me take this valise, I will get right to work on this case. This end will keep me busy for some time, and, if I want any more help I suppose I can see you."

"At any time," replied the president quickly.

Larry emptied the bricks, and their newspaper wrappings, from the satchel. They had played the part of a million dollars most successfully for a time, and they were, to a certain extent, relics of value.

"These had better be saved," spoke the young reporter, wrapping the bricks in the papers and placing them on the president's desk.

"What good will they be?" sneered Mr. Wilson.

"They may come in handy as clews, after I get through with the satchel," replied Larry quietly.

"Humph! This is all nonsense!" exclaimed the black-moustached director. "Besides, Mr. Bentfield, the regular police, or the private detectives, may want this valise as evidence. I don't believe this reporter should take it away."

"The private detectives did not want it," said the president. "They said it was of no help to them, though they did have it photographed in case they might need to refer to it. And I guess the regular detectives will be the same way."

"Any time they want it they can have it," interposed Larry. "I will keep it safe."

"Then you may take it," decided the president. "I'm sure I hope you will be successful."

"It's all nonsense!" declared Mr. Wilson. "No good can come of having a reporter try to solve this mystery! He will put too much news in his paper."

"And publicity is just the thing you need now!" declared Mr. Potter. "If you had made this robbery public at once, our depositors would not have been worried, for at the same time, a reassuring statement could have been made. Then, too, the thief would not have had such a chance to escape. As it is, he has a three days' start with that million."

"I'm not so sure of that," said Larry.

"What do you mean?" asked the president quickly.

"I think," answered the young reporter, "that the thief, and the million, are still in New York city. Of course I may be mistaken, but that is my theory. Now I'm going to see if I can prove it."

"Nonsense! All nonsense!" murmured Mr. Wilson, as Larry left the president's room, carrying the valise.

"Well, now that I've got it, I wonder what I shall do with it?" asked Larry of himself, as he walked down the bank steps. The institution had closed for the day, though a curious crowd was outside, looking at the place from which a million in cash had so mysteriously disappeared. Many in the crowd held copies of the *Leader*, with Larry's story on the front page, but none of them knew that the young man, walking down the steps with a valise in his hand, was the reporter who had sprung the big sensation on the city.

The valise, however, at once attracted attention.

"Hey, dere goes a guy wid money!" cried a newsboy.

"Maybe dat's part ob de million!" added another.

"Hey, mister, lend me ten thousand plunks, will youse?" besought a ragged urchin. "I'll give youse my note fer it!"

The crowd laughed at this, and Larry smiled. He made his way through the press of people, many of whom evidently believed that the valise did contain a large sum. Men began to crowd uncomfortably close up to Larry.

A policeman, of whom there were several in the throng, elbowed his way to the young reporter's side.

"Do you need any help?" he asked, for he had noted that Larry came from the bank. "If there's money in that you ought to have some one with you."

"It's perfectly empty," replied Larry, with a laugh. "See!" and he opened the satchel and held it upside down. There was a craning of necks, as though the crowd expected to see a shower of greenbacks, but they were disappointed.

"He's been robbed, too!" cried a boy laughing, and the crowd joined in. The policeman smiled, nodded at Larry, and then interest in him was over.

"It takes money these days to make a sensation," mused the young reporter as he hurried on. "Now I've got to make some plans. Guess I'll report back to the office, and then go home. I can think better there."

As he hurried up Wall street, toward Broadway, he saw, just coming out from a side entrance to the building in which the looted bank was located, a figure that was vaguely familiar. It was that of a young man of about Larry's build.

"I've seen him before," mused the young reporter. "I wonder where it was. If he turned around—"

As if in answer to Larry's thoughts, the young man ahead of him did turn around, and as soon as our hero had a glimpse of the face he exclaimed:

"The subway shover! That's the man I had the row with—the one who stepped on that girl's foot! No wonder I knew him! I wonder if he'll make trouble?"

But the youth, after a quick glance at Larry—a glance that seemed to be filled with suspicion—hurried on, and he was soon lost in the crowd that now thronged Broadway.

"I'm glad he didn't come back, and demand satisfaction," thought Larry, "though I'd have given it to him if he'd done so. And so we meet again, Mr. Pusher. And, if I'm not mistaken, you came from the Consolidated Bank. I must look you up when I've traced the valise clew as far as it goes. Well, I've got my work cut out for me," and Larry shook his head, for, the more he thought of the bank mystery, the deeper it seemed to become.

CHAPTER VI
UNEXPECTED EVIDENCE

"LARRY, aren't you late to-night?" asked his mother, as, shortly after his talk with the bank directors, the young reporter entered the apartment where he lived. "Oh, are you going out of town?" she inquired, as she caught sight of the valise.

"Bring me somethin' back, Larry?" begged his little sister Mary.

"Take me with you!" exclaimed James, who always wanted to be on the go.

"Are you really going anywhere, Larry?" asked Lucy, the sister who had been cured of a serious spinal ailment by a celebrated doctor, through Larry's suggestion.

"No," he answered, as he kissed them all. "I'm going to stay right here —for a while, anyhow."

"Then why the valise?" asked his mother.

"That," said Larry, with pretended solemnity, "is all that remains of a million dollars."

"A million dollars!" exclaimed Lucy.

"In big bills," added Jerry. "Thousand-dollar bills. Enough to buy this big apartment house in which we live, several times over. Enough to do so many things that it would make your head swim to think of them. And this is all that's left."

"Oh, it's a fairy story! I know it is!" cried James, who was fond of strange tales. "Tell it to me, Larry."

So Larry did, but it was a different story from the one the small lad had expected, though it was none the less interesting.

"And so the million dollars disappeared," concluded Larry, "and this valise and some bricks are all that are left to remember them by."

"And you're going to try to find the money?" asked his mother anxiously. "Oh, Larry! I'm afraid you'll run into some danger."

"What! Danger in trying to find a million dollars?"

"No, but in trying to find the thief," said Mrs. Dexter.

"Well, I haven't found him yet, and maybe I won't," spoke the young reporter. "But I'm going to try, and I don't believe there'll be much danger. As for the money—well, that may never be found."

"What are you going to do with the valise?" asked Lucy.

"It's the first clew I'm working on," replied her brother. "But, now that I have it, I really don't know what to do with it. I'd like to find out where the thief got it."

"Then why don't you go to the stores where they sell such satchels as that, and ask if they sold any lately, and to whom?" suggested Lucy.

"Say! I believe you've struck it!" cried Larry. "That is just what I'll do. I was wondering how I'd get on the track of the person who bought this, and that's the only way. Say, Lucy, I'll make you my first lady assistant," and he laughed at his joke.

"But how can you ever find out, in such a big city as New York, who bought a valise that is just like thousands of others?" asked Mrs. Dexter curiously.

"Only by asking in all the places where they sell them," replied Larry, "and at that, it's a slim chance. But it's worth taking."

He had stopped in the *Leader* office that afternoon, before coming home, and had had a talk with the city editor. Mr. Ember had told Larry to go ahead on his own lines, to do just as he thought best, always remembering that the paper wanted news, above everything else, and exclusive news, or "beats," in preference to any other.

"I think your idea of the valise clew is a good one," the editor had said. "You needn't write too much about it, or the other papers will be on the same trail. But as soon as you find out anything definite, then spring the story."

And so Larry had gone home to puzzle over the matter. Now he had something definite to work on, as a result of Lucy's suggestion, and he determined to begin the first thing in the morning.

Accordingly, after a visit to the office of the paper, when he wrote a short story of his talk with the directors, he started uptown again.

"I'll try the trunk and bag stores first," thought Larry. "This is an expensive sort of valise, made of good leather, and a small store would not be likely to carry it. So I'll try the big places first. It looks like a stock bag, for it doesn't seem as if it had been made to order."

The valise was a yellow one, made of strong, heavy leather, with substantial clasps or handles. It was not such a one as would be purchased by a casual traveler, but looked to be made for carrying heavy weights.

It would be of little interest, and serve no purpose, to detail all of Larry's trips to various stores in search of information as to one that had recently sold a valise such as he carried. Shop after shop was visited without result.

Only a few had ever carried such a satchel as was used to aid in the robbery. Some had sold out their supply years before, and had not replenished it. Others still had some, but had made no sale of them in months. The bags were made in various factories, from a stock pattern, and it was practically impossible to trace the one in question in that way.

"Well, I guess I've covered nearly all the regular bag and trunk stores," said Larry, about a week after he had begun his detective work on the bank mystery. "Now for the department stores. They're going to be harder yet."

All this time nothing very new had developed about the robbery, so there was not much for the young reporter to write for the *Leader*. The story still "ran," but it was mostly of the financial effect, and the efforts of the Consolidated to recoup itself after the big loss. Of his search for the store that had sold the bag Larry wrote nothing, and none of the other papers seemed to be following that clew.

Larry visited many department stores, and at first, as had been the case on his trips to the trunk shops, he met with no success. Not many of the stores carried bags of the kind in question, and few had sold any lately. Of those that had, the sales could be traced, and they were to persons who were above suspicion.

"I guess I'll not do much on this trail," thought Larry, regretfully, as he came out of the store after store without any result. "I'll tackle the bricks next."

He was approaching one of the largest department stores in the city, as these rather gloomy thoughts came to him, and, as he turned down Sixth avenue, to enter it, he wondered if, after all, he would be successful.

As he had done on his visits to other department shops, he went directly to the office of the superintendent.

"I'm from the *Leader*," Larry explained briefly, "and I'd like to know if you handle these bags, and if you sold any lately. It's about the million-dollar bank robbery," he added, as he showed the valise.

"Is that so?" inquired the superintendent interestedly. "Well, say, we do handle those bags. I remember seeing some in the trunk department not long ago. But I guess I'd better refer you to the head of stock. She'll know more about them than I do, and some of the sales people may remember selling such a bag recently. That was a big robbery, all right. Did you write the story of it?"

"I did," admitted Larry modestly.

"Good! I'm glad to have met you. Here, boy, show this gentleman to the trunk department, and tell Miss Mason I said she was to give him any information she had."

Larry followed his guide through the big store, and was soon in the section where traveling bags, trunks and other aids to tourists were displayed.

"Miss Mason! Oh, Miss Mason!" sung out the boy. "Some one to see you."

"Molly! Molly!" cried one of the salesgirls. "You're wanted."

"Molly Mason," mused Larry. "That's a pretty name. I wonder if the young lady is pretty, too? But if she's head of stock most likely she's an elderly lady."

"Miss Mason!" cried the boy again.

"Molly! Molly!" exclaimed the salesgirl.

"Coming," answered a pleasant voice, and Larry started, for he realized that he had heard that voice before. A moment later a young lady—an exceedingly pretty young lady—stood before him, looking at him with wonder in her brown eyes.

"Oh!" she exclaimed. "Oh, you're—" She stopped in some confusion, and blushed.

"Well, this is strange!" cried Tom. "I never thought I'd find you here!"

To his great surprise he found himself confronted by the young lady to whom he had rendered assistance in the subway about a week before—the young lady whom the unmannerly bully had shoved to one side in boarding the train.

"Are you all right now?" asked Larry. "Is—er—does your ankle pain you?"

"Not at all, thank you," she replied, blushing more than ever. There was heard the laughter of several salesgirls, and the messenger boy looked on and grinned. Larry felt himself getting red in the face.

"I—er—I—well, I didn't come here to ask how you were getting on, Miss Mason," stammered Larry. "That is, not exactly, though I was interested in you. I'm Mr. Larry Dexter, from the *Leader*. I'm on this bank mystery case, and this is the valise that was used to turn the trick. I'm trying to find out where it was sold, and who bought it.

"I've tried lots of places, and finally I came here. I have seen the superintendent, and he said it would be all right to interview the head of stock here, though I never expected to meet you."

"Dat's right," put in the boy. "De super says youse is t' tell him all he wants t' know," and then, with a frank wink at Larry, the lad scurried away.

"Well, I'm sure I'll tell you all I can," began Miss Mason. "But I don't know that I can help you. What is it you want to know?"

"Do you recollect selling any bags like this lately?" asked Larry, holding out the one from which he hoped so much.

"Why, yes, I do," was the unexpected answer. "I have sold several lately, and so have the girls in this department. But I don't know that this one is from our stock. Let me look at it."

She opened it, and examined it closely. Then she gave voice to an exclamation:

"That's surely from our stock!" she cried. "It's one I sold myself. I remember it, because the cost mark was blurred," and she showed Larry where, in an obscure place on the lining, there were some letters in ink.

"You sold this very bag?" asked Larry, in delighted surprise.

"Yes."

"When?"

"About two weeks ago. Wait, I can tell you exactly by looking at my memoranda book." She hurried to get it, and, on her return, stated that it was just ten days previous that the valise had been sold.

"Now, if you can only tell me to whom it went, maybe I can get on the trail of the thief," spoke Larry eagerly. "Any record of it, Miss Mason?"

The young lady looked carefully over her book, and then shook her head.

"I'm sorry," she answered, "but that's all I can tell you. Wait a moment, though. There were two of these bags sold that day. I always keep an account of my stock, so I can tell. Two bags were sold. I disposed of one, and Miss Jones, that's the head clerk, of the other."

"But can't you recollect to whom you sold the bag?" asked Larry desperately.

"Wait," begged Miss Mason. She was trying hard to think. "I'm so busy that it's hard to remember all the customers," she said. "But—yes, I have it! I sold that bag to a man! I recollect now. He said he wanted a strong and heavy one, and, after looking at several, he took this one. He wanted a reduction because the leather was chafed, on one corner, and I took off fifty cents. That, and the fact of the cost mark being blurred, makes me remember it now."

"And is there any way of telling to whom Miss Jones sold the other bag?" asked Larry.

"I'll find out," spoke Miss Mason. It did not take long for Miss Jones to show, by her sales slips, that the bag she had disposed of went to a well-known lady customer of the store.

"I guess that lets her out," decided Larry. "But can you recollect what sort of a man it was to whom you sold this valise, Miss Mason?"

The girl was racking her memory, and trying hard to think. Larry was desperately nervous, for he felt, after all his work, that he was at last on the beginning of the trail. Most unexpectedly he had hit upon it.

"Try! Try!" he whispered to Miss Mason.

She smiled at him.

"I'd like to oblige you," she said, "for you were very kind to me. But I don't want to give you misleading information."

"No, that would be worse than none," declared Larry. "But if I could get some sort of description of the man, I might be able to—"

Suddenly Miss Mason clutched the arm of the young reporter. They were alone in an aisle of the trunk department, for the other girls had gone to different parts of the floor.

"Look! Look!" the girl whispered. "If this isn't a coincidence! I never could have described the man to you who purchased that valise, for I haven't a very good memory for faces, but, unless I'm greatly mistaken, there he stands now!"

She pointed to a man with his back toward herself and Larry. A man who, even from this unsatisfactory view, seemed strangely familiar to the young reporter.

"There he is! There's the man who bought the valise!" whispered Miss Mason.

CHAPTER VII
THE CLEW OF THE BRICKS

For a moment Larry did not know what to do. It seemed almost unnatural that, at the very moment when his long quest should have been partly successful, the very man whom, above all others, he wanted to capture, should stand before him.

"Are you sure—very sure?" he whispered to Miss Mason.

"Quite sure," she replied. "I remember because I was alone here at the time, and as I came up from a distant part of the store I saw this man standing here at the pile of valises, examining them. I hurried up to wait on him, for we don't like customers to be kept waiting, and none of the clerks was at hand then. It was then I sold him the valise."

"And you're sure this is the same man?" asked Larry again.

"Almost positive," she replied, still whispering. "I saw his back first, and, though I have not a very good memory for faces, I can very often recognize persons by their forms. I'm sure this is the same man. He has on the same kind of coat, and—"

"I wonder what I'd better do?" interrupted Larry. "If that's the fellow, he had something to do with the robbery, and he ought to be questioned, if nothing more. I wonder if I can send a message to police headquarters from here, and keep watch of that man so he doesn't get away?"

"I'll telephone for you," offered the girl eagerly. "I'd like to do you a favor after what you did for me. You stay here, and watch that man. I'll call up the police. We have branch 'phones on every floor. Wait for me."

Just as she was about to hurry away, and when another moment would have brought about a curious complication of affairs, the man about whom they were talking suddenly turned around. He had been looking at some steamer trunks, and, apparently having about decided on the kind he wanted, he looked around for a clerk to wait on him. This gave Larry and Miss Mason a good view of his face, and the girl in a tense whisper at once exclaimed:

"Oh, Mr. Dexter! I've made a mistake! That isn't the man at all. Oh, don't summon the police!"

"Not the man!" whispered Larry hoarsely.

"No! It looked like him, when he had his back turned, but, now that I see his face, I know he isn't the same one."

"Are you sure?" asked Larry, not wanting to be balked after all his hard work. "Think well, now! Is that the man who bought the valise?"

"No, he isn't the same one," replied the girl. "That man had a beard, and this one is smooth-shaven."

There was no doubt about that, for the man, who had turned and was looking squarely at Larry and the girl, had no sign of beard or moustache. And then Larry gave a gasp.

"Why! Why!" he whispered. "That's the man we met in the subway! The man who jostled you—whom I shoved off the train platform. Don't you remember him?"

"Indeed I do!" exclaimed the girl. "I still limp a little because of him stepping on my foot. But see! He's looking right at us! Oh, what shall I do?"

The mysterious man unexpectedly solved the problem for them, for, no sooner had he caught sight of Larry and the girl, than he gave a start, and turned hurriedly aside. A moment later he fairly ran down an aisle leading toward an elevator.

"Well, what do you think of that?" gasped Larry.

"He was afraid," declared Miss Mason.

"Of me, or you, or—both of us?" asked Larry. "Are you sure he wasn't the man to whom you sold the valise?"

"Almost positive. That man had a black beard."

"It might have been a false one," suggested the reporter.

"I do not think so," the girl answered. "I have been in some amateur theatricals, and I can tell a false beard when I see one. His was real. No, that young man wasn't the one."

"Then why did he run?" asked Larry suspiciously.

"Maybe he thought you would take after him," suggested Miss Mason, with a smile. "He doubtless remembered how you treated him after he jostled against me."

"Well, that may be the reason," agreed Larry, doubtfully.

"I'm sure of it," said Miss Mason.

"Then I guess I'm at the end of my rope," said the young reporter, after a bit. "That wasn't the man who bought the valise, though he looked like him from the back. The one who bought it had a black beard, but as there must be thousands of men in New York who have the same kind of whiskers, that clew isn't of much account. I guess I'll have to go back to the bricks."

"The bricks?" questioned the girl wonderingly.

"Yes, the bricks that took the place of money. They're my next clew. I'll begin work on them. There's no use chasing after that fellow," and he nodded in the direction taken by the rude chap. "Though if I see him in the subway again I'll make him behave. I suppose, Miss Mason, there is no other way of tracing the man who bought this valise?" he asked, after a pause.

"No, it was a cash sale, and he did not give his name. If I could only give you a better description of him!"

"Well, perhaps it wouldn't help much," said Larry. "I'm sure I'm much obliged to you for what you did. Now I'll go back to the bricks. Anyhow, I've got a good story out of it. I don't suppose you want your picture in the paper, as the girl who sold the million-dollar valise."

"Would it help you any?" she asked.

"Indeed it would!" exclaimed Larry fervently.

"Then you may have it, though I don't like publicity," she replied. "But I haven't one here."

"I'll call at your house for it," said Larry quickly, and thus he got her address.

Larry wrote a good article, and of course secured a "beat" out of the valise story. It was run with Miss Mason's picture, and made quite a sensation, being copied by the other less fortunate papers.

But now, indeed, Larry seemed "at the end of his rope." The valise clew had ended in a blind lead, for naturally it was out of the question to seek a man with a black beard, and with no other description to go by.

Still, Larry looked over all the men employed by the bank that had been robbed. None of them had black beards, and he was farther off from the trail than ever. But he did settle one important point, and that was the knowledge that the man who had acted so rudely in the subway was a messenger employed by the Consolidated National.

This man, whose name Larry learned was Harrison Witherby, was employed as a "runner." That is, he took checks, notes, bills, and so forth, from his bank to others, or to the Clearing House, where, each day, banks in New York exchange their depositors' checks put in for collection, for drafts on their own bank, and so strike a balance.

Witherby was not in the bank much, and that is how it happened that Larry had not before noticed him. His duties kept him busy outside.

"And so he's the man with whom I had the run-in," mused the young reporter. "Well, the less I have to do with him the better. Now to see what I can do with the bricks."

Naturally, President Bentfield was disappointed when Larry reported that the valise clew had amounted to nothing.

"Well, keep on," he advised the young reporter.

"I will," promised Larry. "Something may turn up later. Have you heard anything?"

"Not a thing. The police seem completely baffled. We have every employee under strict watch, but it has resulted in nothing. None of them has gone away, or shown any inclination to leave. Their records are perfect as far as we can learn. It is a great mystery."

"Well, I'll see what clew the bricks give me," spoke Larry.

"You'll find them in the closet where the valise was," said the president, who was on his way out of his office. "Go right in, Larry. My private office is open."

The young reporter stepped in, carrying the valise from which he had hoped so much, but which had only proved a baffling clew. He tossed it into the closet, and picked up the bundle of bricks, in their newspaper wrappings. He intended to take them home to look at them. Later he intended on calling at a number of brick yards to learn, if possible, where the bricks had come from.

As he was going out of the president's office he almost collided with a young man, and a moment's glance showed Larry that it was Witherby, the uncouth runner.

"Oh, I—er—I didn't know you were here!" exclaimed the young man with whom our hero had had the encounter in the subway. "What are you doing in the president's private office?"

"He told me to go there," said Larry coldly, not caring to give his real reason.

"That's right," spoke the president's private messenger, coming up at this moment. "Mr. Dexter was sent in here to get—"

"To get some private papers!" exclaimed Larry quickly, with a wink at the messenger. The latter was in the confidence of the president, and it had been agreed that Larry's mission was to be kept as secret as possible from the other bank employees.

"Oh, all right," stammered Witherby. "I—"

"Did *you* want anything?" asked the messenger quickly.

"I—er—Director Wilson asked me to see if Mr. Bentfield was in," was the stammering answer. "He wants to see the president."

"Well, Mr. Bentfield has gone for the day," spoke the messenger. "Good afternoon, Mr. Dexter," and he ushered out Larry, who carried the load of bricks, while Harrison Witherby, with a black look at our hero, went back to his own department.

CHAPTER VIII
BAFFLED

"WHAT would happen if any one met me, and saw what I had in this package," mused Larry, as he walked up Wall street with the bricks in their newspaper wrappings under his arms. "If some of the police, or detectives, who are working on this bank mystery, happened to see me come out of the Consolidated building with this package they'd surely think I was a new kind of a confidence man, or a gold-brick swindler.

"Or they might take me for an up-to-date hod-carrier," he added, with a smile. "Well, being a reporter makes you do all sorts of queer jobs, but I like it. I only hope I can solve this mystery, and get the thief. And suppose I recovered the money? A million dollars!"

The idea was so tremendous that Larry lost himself for a moment in thinking of it, as he neared the busy throngs on Broadway. Then another thought flashed into his mind.

"Twenty thousand dollars reward," he said softly. "If I should get that, or even half of it, I could afford to get out of the newspaper game. And yet I don't know as I would. There is too much excitement in it. I like it. And I might get at least ten thousand dollars, if I found the thief. I might have to divide with some one who helped me arrest him, for I could hardly take him into custody alone.

"Oh, but what's the use of thinking about it until I've got more of a clew than I have at present?" he asked himself. "Well, maybe the bricks will help me, but it's a pretty slim chance."

Larry, however, was used to taking slim chances, as indeed most reporters are, and so he was not going to get discouraged before he had even started on the new trail. There were many things to think of, and he began on some new lines.

"I wonder why that fellow Witherby comes across my path so often?" mused Larry. "I don't like him. Not because he acted so toward Miss Mason, in the subway, but because there is something suspicious about him. He always acts as though he was afraid of me.

"Maybe that's because I hauled him off the platform. But he's bigger than I am, and he ought to be able to trim me in a fight. Though I wouldn't be afraid of him. I can't understand it."

Larry shook his head over the problems he was called on to solve, but still he liked the hard work.

"And, come to think of it, there's something else," went on Larry, who had a habit of thinking things out in detail; a habit formed by his experience as a reporter. "Witherby and Director Wilson seem to be quite friendly. Mr. Wilson sends Witherby in to see if President Bentfield is in his office, or—"

Larry came to a sudden stop, as a new idea came to him.

"Maybe Mr. Wilson wasn't in the bank just now, after all!" the young reporter said, half aloud. "Come to think of it, he wouldn't be very likely to be there so late. And, if he was, he'd come in to see the president by the private door, opening from the corridor, and not through the clerk's cage. By Jove! I believe Witherby made that yarn up. He wanted an excuse to come into the president's office, to see what I was up to, and he took that one. There's something wrong about Witherby, I'm sure.

"But I've got to keep quiet about it. I'll just work up that clew. Still, come to think of it, he and Mr. Wilson are a bit friendly. I've often seen them talking together.

"Pshaw! I guess I'd better try one thing at a time. I'll see what the bricks can do for me," and, with this idea, Larry hurried to get home as soon as possible, and map out a plan of campaign.

"Well, Larry," exclaimed his mother, when he came in and put the bricks on the table, "are you going into the building business?"

"Oh, he's going to play blocks with me; aren't you, Larry?" asked little Mary eagerly.

"Of course!" laughed Larry, catching her up in his arms and kissing her. "You can build a little house by yourself, Mary, while I look over these papers, and then I'll build a house for you."

The bricks, which had been found in the substituted valise, were not the ordinary kind. They were somewhat smaller, and of the variety known as pressed-glazed. They were used in the better class of houses, to make a neat appearance around the kitchen range or in bathrooms, and on the side walls of restaurants. There were quite a number of them, for they were smaller than the ordinary red brick.

Mary began building a "house" with them, when Larry had put them on the floor for her, and the young reporter carefully looked at the newspapers in which the specimens of building material had been wrapped.

If he had hoped for a clew from the prints he was disappointed, for there were several sheets of a New York paper, with nothing on them to distinguish them from thousands of other sheets of the same date.

"But the date may help some," thought Larry, noting that the paper had been issued a few days before the robbery took place.

44

"Whoever wrapped up the bricks probably took the first paper that was handy," mused the reporter. "If he picked up the bricks at some building he either found a paper in the street to wrap them in, or he had a paper in his pocket. The latter is most likely to be the case, for if a fellow intended to rob a bank, and needed bricks to represent the weight of money, he wouldn't go about a new building in the daytime and pick them up. He'd wait until after dark, so he would not be seen.

"And by the same reasoning, he wouldn't take a chance on finding a paper near the building. Of course he *might* find one, but it would be likely to be dirty. So he'd carry a paper with him in his pocket, all ready to wrap the bricks in."

When Larry had reasoned matters thus far he had to admit that the paper itself was a pretty slim clew. All it gave him was the date, but that suggested something new.

"Let's see," mused the young reporter. "The date of the paper is the same as the day when Miss Mason sold the mysterious man the valise. She sold it to him late in the afternoon. The fellow must have gone from the store to some building, picked up the bricks after dark, and taken them home with him. Then, at the proper time, he took the fake bag and the bricks to the bank and 'switched' the poor valise for the rich one, making himself a million dollars richer by the exchange.

"That means that it was some one in the bank who turned the trick, and there's no getting away from that. But who was it? That's the point, and where is the money? For it's a moral certainty that the fellow hasn't skipped with it, since no one has quit the bank's employment since the robbery. The thief is still connected with the bank, and the money is hidden somewhere. It's up to me to find it."

That was as far as Larry could go. His brain was tired with much thinking, and, putting aside the paper, he got down on the floor to play "blocks" with his little sister Mary. As he built castles, towers, palaces and just plain houses, he looked carefully at the bricks. He was planning some way of finding who made them, and at what building they would likely have been taken from.

That night, when the children had gone to bed, Larry went out to the nearest drug store, and came back with a directory.

"Now what are you doing?" asked his mother.

"Looking up all the firms who make this kind of brick," he replied. "I'm going to call on as many as I can to-morrow."

This plan he put in operation, but it was a baffling search. He found that the bricks in question were made by only one firm, which he located after calling on a number. But here the clew failed.

"We have sold thousands of those bricks," said the manager, to whom the young reporter applied after showing a sample of the bricks taken from the valise. "Yes, I might say half a million of them. They have been delivered to dozens of builders in New York City, and the outskirts, and used in a variety of ways. One brick is as like another as are two peas, and it would be out of the question to try to trace where the few were picked up that took the place of the million dollars."

"Yes, I'm afraid so," agreed Larry. "This is the end of this clew all right," and, tired and discouraged, he started back for the office of the *Leader*, there to write for the next day a story of his baffling search.

CHAPTER IX
LARRY GOES WALKING

THE brick story made good reading, even if it was but a record of failure, and, for that matter, almost anything that was printed about the great bank mystery was eagerly pored over by the general public.

Larry's account of how he sought to establish a clew by the bricks was another "beat," and many city editors of other papers administered severe rebukes to their reporters, who were covering the bank story, because they had not thought to try that means of solving the mystery.

"How did you do it, Larry?" asked Peter Manton, with a rueful countenance, for Peter was one of those who had been "called down" for failing to get a good story of the developments of the robbery.

"Oh, just by thinking," answered Larry, with a laugh.

"What are you going to do next?" Peter wanted to know. "Though of course I don't expect you to tell me," he added, with a sigh at his failure.

"Well, to tell you the truth, I don't know what I *am* going to do next," replied Larry. "I don't know what there is to do. I'm at the end of my rope again. The brick clew failed, just as the others did. But I'm not going to give up."

Indeed, it was hard to know what next step to take. Larry had several talks with his city editor, who suggested some new ideas. President Bentfield, likewise, was appealed to, but he could offer nothing new.

"All we want, Larry, is to get the thief," he said. "And the money, too, if you can, for though the directors have made good the loss, it was a heavy blow to them."

"Are the police and private detectives still seeking clews, and investigating the records of the different clerks and employees?" asked Larry.

"Yes, and I might say that the police are rather put out at me for allowing you to work on the case. I fancy, though, that they are nettled because they did not think to try the valise and brick clews, and you got all the credit for that I'm not going to take you off the case, though, Larry, so don't worry."

"Well, the valise clew didn't amount to any more than the brick one did," said the reporter ruefully, "though it did bring out the fact that a man with a black beard bought the satchel. And you have no bearded employees in the bank."

"Only myself," admitted the president, with a smile, "and my beard is white. I didn't dye it in order to purchase the valise, either," he added laughing.

"Of course the real thief might have had a confederate purchase the valise for him," suggested Larry. "And that makes it all the harder. Miss Mason gave me all the help she could, but she did not take much notice of the man, except that he looked like Harrison Witherby from the back."

"Not a very safe clew to go on," commented the bank president. "Besides, Mr. Witherby is one of our most trusted employees, and has been with us for years. I would as soon think of suspecting myself as him."

Larry did not impose such unbounded confidence in the clerk who had proved himself such a bully, but he did not care to tell Mr. Bentfield this. Nor, in fact, had the young reporter come to the point of seriously suspecting Witherby. Larry was only "keeping his eyes open."

Several days passed, the detectives meanwhile using all their skill to unearth the thief, or discover the hiding-place of the million dollars. Naturally, to be under observation, as the bank employees were all the while, made them feel unpleasant, but there was no help for it, and they accepted it with the best grace possible. There was a mutual feeling of distrust and annoyance, for it had now come to be accepted as a fact that if some one actually employed in the bank had not taken the money, at least they had aided in its disappearance. Still, there was no change in the situation, and every clerk, teller and cashier stayed at his post.

"That thief, whoever he is, has the best nerve of any one I ever heard off," thought Larry one day, after a visit to Mr. Bentfield. The young reporter looked into the brass "cage" where the clerks were, wondering which of them would finally prove to have been concerned in the robbery.

At this moment Witherby looked up, and, catching Larry's glance, he frowned. A little later, just as Larry was going out, Director Wilson entered, and the reporter heard him tell a messenger that he wanted to speak to Witherby.

"They're getting thicker than ever," mused Larry. "But I don't know that it has any significance. Mr. Wilson hasn't much use for me, and he laughed at my efforts. But so far I've showed that I was partly right, and, before I'm through with this case, I'll show him that I'm altogether right. But what shall I do next?"

It was a hard question to answer. In lieu of something better to do Larry called at police headquarters, where he was well known. He found several friends there, one of whom, Detective Nyler, had done some work on the bank mystery.

"Larry, what are you going to pull off next?" asked Nyler, who had followed Larry's stories in the *Leader* closely. "You are putting it all over us down here. What's next?"

"I don't know, Billy. I wish I did. I thought maybe I could get some points from you."

"Nothing doing. I'm off that case now. Working on a good second-story job, though. When I get my man I'll give you the story."

"Thanks. Anything else new?"

"No; but say, Larry, if I were you I'd keep on with that brick end of the game a little longer."

"What's the use? Those bricks might have been picked up at any one of fifty buildings. I never could find which one, and, if I did, what good would it do me?"

"Larry, I think there's just one point you overlooked," said Detective Bill Nyler earnestly.

"What?" asked Larry eagerly.

"Well, I'll grant that you're a better detective than lots that are in the business," went on the headquarters man, "but you've still something to learn. Now, I read in the paper about how you played the brick end of it up, but you didn't go quite far enough with it."

"Why not?"

"Look here. It's pretty certain, isn't it, that the man who 'switched' the satchel full of money, for one with bricks in, prepared the dummy valise outside the bank?"

"Sure. That's easy to guess."

"Then where did he do it? Not at the corner of Broadway and Wall street, that's sure. He'd pick out the most secluded place he could find, and that would be his own room.

"Now then, there are several fellows who work in the Consolidated Bank. Any one of them may have committed this robbery, and, again, it may have been done by some clever outsider, though I'm not strong on that theory. If it was a bank clerk he fixed that bag up in his room. A room is in a house—which, though it sounds like a lesson in the first reading book, isn't so simple as it seems.

"What I mean is, that the thief wouldn't go too far from his room in order to get the bricks. He'd pick out some place as near his house, and room, as possible."

"Why?" asked Larry.

"So as to make the chance of him being seen with the bricks so much less. He picked up the bricks at some building at night, you say, and I believe it."

"There's hardly a doubt of that," spoke Larry. "For he wouldn't risk going up in an open manner and asking some mason for the bricks. Whoever he asked for them would have remembered it, when the story came out, and we'd have more evidence—which we now haven't. So I believe he took the bricks at night, from some building, without asking any one."

"Of course," agreed the detective, "and he'd want to travel as short a distance afterward as possible. For, look you, Larry, a fellow with a load of bricks might meet a policeman, or a detective, who, naturally, would be suspicious. So I think the thief just slipped out of his house, went a short distance, picked up the bricks, and skipped back."

"By Jove! I never thought of that!" exclaimed Larry. "You mean—"

"I mean that you ought to get a list, showing where every employee of the bank lives. Then take a walk around each of their houses, and see if there isn't a new building going up near some of them, where these bricks are being used. Then you may have something to work on."

"I will!" cried Larry, the light of a new hope shining in his eyes. "This is great, Bill! I guess I've got lots to learn, after all. I will take a walk around, and keep my eyes open."

"There's only one trouble," suggested the detective, with a twinkle in his eyes; "you may find half a dozen new houses with these bricks scattered about them, and some bank employee may live near each one. Then you'll have six fellows to be suspicious of."

"That's better than having a whole bankful," replied the young reporter. "I'm off now."

His first care was to get from Mr. Bentfield a list of the residences of all the bank employees. Nor would he say why he wanted it. Then Larry began a sort of walking tour, intending to cover a good part of New York. He would first locate the house of some employee, and then circle about it to find a building in course of erection—a building where the bricks were used that had played such a part in the robbery. "Million-dollar bricks," Larry called them, and it is as good a term as any other to employ in describing them.

"Well, this may make a good story, even if I don't get any real clew out of it," mused Larry, as he began his walk.

CHAPTER X
AN UNEXPECTED MEETING

LARRY DEXTER'S task was not an easy one. In the first place there were nearly a hundred of the bank employees, about whose houses he had to circle, in order to determine if there were any of the million-dollar bricks in the vicinity. This in itself was tedious work, but Larry was eager on the trail, for he could not tell at what moment he might make an unexpected discovery.

A week went by, however, with no result. Larry had "covered" many of the residences of the employees, but near none of them were buildings in the course of erection, where the bricks in question could be found.

The young reporter had his own troubles, too, for in several cases, after locating a new building near some bank employee's house, and inquiring whether the pressed bricks were being used, he was regarded with suspicion.

More than once he was looked upon as a sort of drummer for the bricks, and told to be off about his own affairs. Again, he was suspected of being a walking delegate, trying to bring about a strike, on account of the use of non-union material, and the foremen were on the point of escorting him off the premises with force.

For, on this search, Larry did not describe himself as a reporter looking for clews in the great bank mystery. He did not want it known who he was, for he realized that if the other papers learned about his efforts they would put reporters on the same scent, and Larry would lose all chance of securing a "beat." And, while he was doing his best to solve the mystery for the bank, his first duty was to his own paper, and he realized that. He must get the "story" if everything else failed. But he hoped he could do both.

It was a warm Sunday in May. All the week Larry had worked hard on the bank mystery, and, now that he had a day of rest, he felt that he wanted to get far away, where he could see nothing to remind him of it, where he could not smell printer's ink, or hear the thunder of the presses, and the rustle of paper.

For, though the young reporter was loyal to his assignment, he realized that sometimes to get away from a case you are hard at work on, and take in new ideas and scenes, helps to bring results when the loose threads of clews are again taken up.

"I think I'll go for a walk in Central Park," he said to his mother, when they had come back from church. "It will do me good. I'll take Mary and James with me."

"No, Larry," suggested his mother. "You just go off by yourself. Lucy will take the little ones. You want to be free to think, and, if you see anything that will help you, you want to be in a position to go after it. Go off by yourself, and maybe you will discover something that will help you."

"All right," he agreed, and so he went for the walk, a walk differing from his usual weekday one, when he was continuously on the lookout for a house where a bank clerk lived, which house might be near a pile of the "million-dollar" bricks.

It was beautiful in the park. As Larry walked along the big gray squirrels scampered about over the green grass, for they are allowed to run free in the big enclosure.

Larry bought a bag of peanuts, and, as he crossed over a roadway, and reached the other side, a big squirrel sat up with tail erect, and eyed him hungrily.

"Peanuts, eh? Want some peanuts?" asked Larry, and, holding out one in his hand toward the squirrel, he was rather surprised when the nimble little creature scrambled up his leg, as though it was the trunk of a tree, thence to his shoulder and along his arm to his outstretched hand, and took the peanut in its paws. Then, as fearless as a kitten, the squirrel sat up on Larry's shoulder, and ate the nut.

"Well, well!" he laughed. "This is a new one on me. I never knew the squirrels were so tame."

They are, as a matter of fact, for kind treatment, and the way the New York boys and girls feed them, has made them so.

Suddenly there was a movement on the path back of Larry. With a frisk of its tail the squirrel scampered down Larry's leg, and ran across the grass, with part of the peanut in its paws. Then there came a girlish laugh, and a voice exclaimed:

"Oh, this is a new part for a reporter to play! Are you getting a story about the tameness of squirrels, Mr. Dexter?"

Larry wheeled about, and saw the girl to whom he had been of service in the subway—the girl who had helped him on the satchel clew—Miss Molly Mason.

"Oh, good afternoon!" he greeted her. "This is an unexpected pleasure. I didn't know you walked in such a prosaic place as Central Park."

"There, or Bronx Park, every pleasant Sunday," she replied, her brown eyes dancing with the joy of the beautiful day. "I am kept in the store so much that I take every chance I get to see the trees, and the green grass."

"So do I," said Larry, walking along at her side. "Are you going anywhere in particular?"

"I am—yes," she answered, and there was a smile on her lips.

"Oh, then don't let me keep you," spoke Larry, a bit stiffly.

"I am going to feed the elephants peanuts," she answered, with a laugh. "I do it every Sunday."

"Oh, then, perhaps you won't mind if I come along," went on the young reporter. "I have some peanuts left, and—well, I am fond of elephants."

"Come on," she challenged. "There is one big fellow that seems to know me. Or else it's the peanuts I bring him."

"I should prefer to think it was yourself," said Larry boldly. "Well, we'll see what the elephant thinks of my peanuts," and they walked along together, laughing and chatting like two children.

Larry felt light-hearted and care-free. He had almost forgotten about the bank mystery, and how much depended on him to solve it, until Miss Mason asked him:

"Have you found the black-bearded man, who bought the valise of me?"

"No, and I'm afraid I never shall," was his answer. "It is a strange mystery. I can't seem to get anywhere with it."

"I wish I could help you," she said earnestly, "but I can't seem to."

"You gave me a good story, at any rate," retorted Larry. "By the way, the art department sent me up your picture to return to you, but—er—do you mind if I keep it for myself?"

She looked at him a moment and answered:

"No—not very much."

"Then I will," exclaimed Larry. "Here we are at the elephant house. Let's see who can feed the big fellows the most peanuts," and, still like children, they entered.

The question of who was the greatest favorite of the pachyderms was not settled. Certain it was that the biggest elephant seemed to like Miss Mason's peanuts better than Larry's, but perhaps that was because she fed them to him by the half-bagful. Soon the two had handed over all the dainties they had purchased.

As they walked up a path Larry saw two figures approaching them. Both were vaguely familiar to him, and he was just wondering who they were, when, suddenly, he came face to face with them.

Even in the waning light he had no trouble in recognizing them. They were Miss Grace Potter, the daughter of the millionaire whom Larry had located after such a search, and Harrison Witherby, the clerk in the Consolidated National Bank, which had been robbed of a million dollars.

"Oh, good evening, Mr. Dexter," greeted Miss Potter, in some surprise, as she noted Larry's companion.

"Good evening," replied the young reporter, and though he glanced at her escort, and nodded, Witherby did not respond, but looked at our hero almost with a sneer.

A moment later and the two couples had passed each other, but Larry's heart was still beating over the unexpected meeting.

CHAPTER XI
THE PILE OF BRICKS

"OH, LARRY—I mean Mr. Dexter—do you know her?" asked Molly Mason, when she was out of earshot from the couple she and her escort had just passed.

"Yes, she is Miss Grace Potter," replied the young reporter. "But you spoke as though you knew her yourself."

"Oh, no, I don't know her, of course. She and I don't move in exactly the same society circle," spoke Miss Mason, with a frank laugh. "But I've often seen her in our store—you notice that I say *our* store," she added, still laughing. "But all we girls always say that. It makes it sound as though we had some interest in it."

"And so Miss Potter comes there?" asked Larry.

"Yes, and the girls all like her, because she is so kind, and considerate. She never makes a fuss, even though she is a millionaire's daughter. You know her father is very rich," she added, for Larry's benefit.

"Oh, yes, I know," he said. "I have good reason to," and he told something about his hunt after the missing millionaire, as I have set it down in the book before this one, called "Larry Dexter's Great Search."

"Then you must know her quite well," went on Miss Mason.

"I do," replied Larry, and he fancied there was just a note of jealousy in his companion's voice. "I met her quite often some time ago, and she was very kind to me, though I was only a reporter, and she a millionaire's daughter."

"That's what the girls in the store say of her," spoke Miss Mason. "You'd never know she had all the money she wanted to spend, to judge by her manner. Some of the very rich people make it hard for working girls," she went on. "They seem to think we have no feelings. But Miss Potter is very different. I wish there were more like her."

"Did you notice who was with her?" asked Larry.

"Not particularly. I saw that it was a young man, not bad-looking. He was—why, of course!" suddenly exclaimed Miss Mason. "I know now what you mean! I was wondering why his face was so familiar. He was the one who jostled me in the subway train that day; wasn't he?" and she leaned eagerly toward Larry.

"The very same," he answered quietly.

"I wonder what he was doing with Miss Potter," went on Larry's companion. "I can't say much about his manners. But perhaps he acts differently toward millionaires' daughters than he does toward working girls."

"I don't doubt it," remarked our hero grimly. He, too, was wondering what had brought Miss Potter and Witherby together. And, though Larry tried not to let himself be conscious of it, he was aware of a distinct pang of jealousy.

"It must be because Mr. Potter banks at the Consolidated and Witherby works there," reasoned Larry to himself. "Though how a bank clerk, on a comparatively small salary, can afford to go around with a millionaire's daughter, is beyond me. But I guess it's none of my business."

"It's queer we should meet that man again," went on Miss Mason, referring to Witherby. "I have often looked for him in the subway, but I've never seen him since that morning."

"I have met him several times," spoke Larry. "He is employed in the Consolidated Bank."

"Where the million-dollar robbery took place?"

"Yes, the same bank."

"And do you suspect him? Oh, Mr. Dexter, maybe he had something to do with it!" exclaimed the girl impulsively.

"Oh, I guess not," laughed Tom. "He doesn't seem to have been in a position where he could have changed the bags, though of course it's possible. I'm beginning to think that the million dollars vanished up the chimney, like smoke, and that the money and the thief will never be found."

"Oh, you mustn't give up so soon," urged Miss Mason.

"I'm not, but I'm just beginning to lose hope."

She and Larry walked on for some little distance farther, and then the young reporter took Miss Mason home, remaining to pay a brief call on her mother.

"Well, I'm going to do something to-morrow," said Larry to himself, as he started for his own home.

And that something was nothing more or less than to visit the vicinity of the house where Witherby lived, and look about it for a tell-tale pile of bricks.

Up to this point Larry had only made his search around the houses, or boarding-places, of those clerks who lived in New York city proper. He intended to gradually extend his field, as some of the employees lived out of town. This was the case with Witherby, whose home was in Hackenford, New Jersey.

"I'll go out to Hackenford to-morrow," decided Larry. "I might as well settle this thing one way or the other as soon as possible. Though I don't understand why, if he lives in Hackenford; he took the subway downtown to New York. Though he might have stayed in the city over-night I guess there's nothing suspicious in that."

Early the next morning Larry went to the office of the *Leader*. He had a "tip" on a story he wanted to turn in, and he wanted to talk with Mr. Emberg, and explain where he was going.

"Well, keep right on with the case," the city editor urged him.

"I'm afraid it's going to fall flat," remarked Larry. "I can't seem to land anything. Do you think it's worth while spending more money on it?"

"I certainly do!" was the quick reply. "We'll get a big story out of it some day. Don't give up, Larry! We haven't lost confidence in you."

"But I'm not grinding out much copy."

"No, but you will. Go on out to Hackenford, and see what turns up."

So Larry took a train for the New Jersey town.

He had no difficulty in locating the place where Witherby lived. It was a small boarding-house, as was evidenced by the sign telling of furnished rooms to let.

"Now to see if there are any of the million-dollar bricks around here," said Larry softly, as, with the boarding-house as a starting point, he set out.

He went up and down many streets looking for new structures. He found several, not far from the place where Witherby lived, but at none of them had the bricks in question been used.

Finally Larry found himself in a street directly back of the one on which the boarding-house was located. And, greatly to the surprise of the young reporter, there was a new building going up in the rear of the place where Witherby lived.

"Now to see if any of the million-dollar bricks are used here," mused Larry, as he approached the structure. "If there are, which the chances are against, it would have been an easy thing for him to have skipped over the back fence some night, gotten the bricks, and jumped back again without any one seeing him."

As he neared the building, he looked about for a sight of the bricks in question, but saw none. Knowing from past experiences, however, that there might be bricks in the cellar, or piled on the floor in one of the rooms, he walked up the improvised steps, and entered. Carpenters and masons were busy on all sides, but they paid no attention to him. Larry strolled through to the kitchen of the house.

And there, on the floor in front of the range, was a pile of enameled bricks—the same sort that had replaced the million dollars in the valise!

"By Jove!" cried Larry. "I've found what I've been looking for! I've found the pile of bricks that are near a house where a bank clerk lives!"

For a moment his heart beat so fast that it seemed as if it would choke him. And then, though he realized that his clew might mean much, he knew that there was still much to be done, to clinch the robbery on Witherby.

"He may be as innocent as I am," thought Larry. "I've got to go slow. It wouldn't be fair to print a story to the effect that he lives near some of the million-dollar bricks, until I've gotten more proof."

He looked out of the window of the unfinished kitchen. In full view was the rear of the house where the suspected bank clerk lived, and, as Larry gazed out, he saw a sight which startled him.

Standing at a window of one of the rear rooms of the boarding-house was a man, a man whose face Larry could see was smooth-shaven. But, even as Larry watched he saw the man fit on his lower jaw a big, black, false beard. Then he looked in the glass as if to note the effect. Larry saw the whole scene plainly.

"By Jove!" whispered the young reporter to himself. "I believe I'm on the trail at last! There is the man with the black beard, and here are the bricks that are like those in the valise! What's my next move? The trail is getting hot!"

CHAPTER XII
TANGLED UP

For a few minutes Larry stood in the kitchen of the unfinished house, looking out of the window at the casement of the boarding-house establishment in the rear—at the window of which stood a man trying on a false beard.

"If I only had thought to bring a pair of opera-glasses, I could see who that man is," mused Larry. "I'll carry them after this. But perhaps I can find out who occupies that room by asking the landlady. I can make some inquiries about rates, and she may think I'm a prospective lodger, and show me through the place. Then I may meet the man. I might meet Witherby, too, and that wouldn't be so pleasant. He might make a row, and stir things up. But I've got to do something."

Larry narrowly watched the man, who could not seem to get the false beard adjusted to his satisfaction. But the young reporter was not in a good position to see the man's face. What glimpses he had of it did not show him any one whom he could recognize.

"Though of course it might be Witherby himself," mused Larry. "He lives there, and that's just as likely to be his room, as that of any one else. I'll go up to the second floor of this house, and see if I can't get a better view of that room and the man in it."

As Larry started from the kitchen he cast a last, hasty glance at the strange man. The young reporter saw him take off the false beard, and, the next moment pull down the shade of the window.

"It's all up now," thought Larry. "I'll have to try some other plan. Guess I'll stay here a while, and see what happens."

But he could not carry out that plan, for a moment later a man, evidently one of the building contractors, entered the kitchen. He looked suspiciously at Larry.

"What are you doing here?" he asked gruffly.

"Looking around," answered Larry coolly.

"Did any one give you permission to come in?"

"No, I just invited myself."

"Are you connected with the owner of this place?"

"No, I don't even know his name."

"Then you'd better be off. We don't like strangers around here. We've been missing things lately."

"Are you accusing me?" asked Larry sharply.

"Well, you can take it as you like. Get out of here, that's all."

"Of course that's your privilege," answered Larry, keeping his temper by an effort; "but I can assure you that I only came here to look around. I am interested in those enameled bricks you are using."

"Agent for 'em?" demanded the contractor. "If you are, I'll say that the bricks are not what they are cracked up to be."

"I'm not the agent," replied Larry, with a smile, and then, for fear the contractor might ask other questions, which would be hard to answer under the circumstances, the young reporter hurried away.

"Let's see," he murmured, as he walked up the street. "I think the next move will be to apply at the boarding-house. Maybe the landlady will answer some questions that will help me solve the mystery."

Larry found the boarding mistress pleasant enough. She doubtless thought she saw in the young reporter a prospective lodger.

"Yes," she said, in answer to his questions, "I have several vacant rooms, and my rates are reasonable."

"Are there other young men here?" asked Larry.

"Oh, yes, several. I have one bank clerk—"

"Mr. Witherby?" interrupted the reporter.

"Yes; how did you know?"

"Oh, I have met him in New York," replied Larry evasively. "Perhaps you would show me some of your rooms."

The landlady was willing, and soon was escorting our hero through the house.

"Is this room occupied?" asked Larry, as he reached the door of the one in which, from the vacant house, he had seen the man with the false beard.

"Yes, Mr. Witherby has that," was the unexpected answer.

"Mr. Witherby!"

Larry started, and he feared lest his voice should have betrayed his anxiety. So Witherby, after all, was the man with the false beard! His house was near the pile of tell-tale bricks. More and more, everything seemed to point to him as the thief.

"Here is a room you might like to look at," said the boarding mistress, opening the door of a chamber some distance down the hall. "I'll just see if it's fit to be inspected." She vanished within the room, while Larry started toward it. At that moment the door of Witherby's apartment opened.

The young reporter swung around to face the bank clerk, but to his surprise he saw a young man, with a sandy moustache, come out—a young man who did not at all resemble the bank clerk, and who looked at Larry with no sign of recognition.

The man with the sandy moustache passed down the hall toward the stairs, and, at that moment the landlady, coming out of the vacant room, saw him.

"Why—why," she stammered. "Who—who are you? I—I did not let you in!"

"He came out of Mr. Witherby's room," explained Larry quickly.

"Then he's a sneak-thief!" cried the landlady sharply. "Call the police! Hold him! He's a thief!"

Larry thought the same thing, the more so as he had seen the performance with the false beard.

"I'll get him!" cried the young reporter.

He darted after the man with the sandy moustache, but the latter, with a quickness that was almost incredible, ran down the stairs. A moment afterward the front door slammed shut behind him, and when Larry reached the stoop there was no one in sight.

"Well, by Jove!" exclaimed the astonished reporter. "That was sure a quick get-away! I wonder where he went?"

"Did you get him? Where is he?" panted the landlady. "Call the police."

"There's not much use of that now," replied the practical Larry. "The fellow has disappeared. He must have run around in some yard, and he's far enough off by this time. The best thing to do would be to see if he has taken anything."

"And to think that he was in Mr. Witherby's room!" lamented the boarding mistress. "Oh, how can I explain it to him? I was sure Mr. Witherby had come home, too, but he must have gone out again. Oh, perhaps this thief has killed him in his room!"

"Not much danger of that," replied Larry. "We'll take a look."

"Oh, I'm so frightened!" cried the woman. "There's no one home now, for my servant has gone to the store. Oh, call the police! I have a telephone."

"Wait until we see if we need them," suggested Larry. "There's no use causing unnecessary excitement. Perhaps you can tell, by looking at Mr. Witherby's room, whether anything is missing."

They found the door locked, but the landlady had a duplicate key, and soon opened it. Nothing appeared disturbed.

"His clothes all seem to be here," said the boarding mistress, as she looked in a closet. "Of course some things may be missing, but we can't tell until Mr. Witherby comes home. Oh, to think of a sneak-thief being in my house!"

"What makes you think Mr. Witherby came home?" asked the young reporter, making up his mind to say nothing of the man with the false beard.

"Because I heard some one come in, and he walked just as my lodger does. Some one went upstairs to Mr. Witherby's room. You know he often comes out this way on banking business, and then he stops in his room. He's often done it, and of course I thought it was him this time. Oh, dear!"

"Well, I wouldn't worry," advised Larry. "The person you heard come in was probably a sneak-thief, who used a skeleton key. He didn't appear to be carrying much away with him, at any rate."

"I can't tell how much my boarders may have been robbed of until they come home," the landlady said. "Oh, what a disgrace to my house!"

"It is too bad," admitted Larry, "but perhaps he got nothing. He was probably frightened by hearing us in the hall. I'll stop on my way down the street and send up the first policeman I meet, if you wish."

"I wish you would," said the woman. "I'd feel safer." Larry concluded this was a good chance for him to get away without again bringing up the matter of engaging a room, and so he hurried out. He met an officer, and, briefly describing the case, advised him to call at the boarding-house.

"Well, things are getting tangled up more than ever," thought the young reporter, as he walked toward the railroad station. "Witherby lives near some of the million-dollar bricks, and he had a chance to use them. But did he? That's the question.

"Then there's this false-beard business and the sneak-thief, though I suppose they only make one clew together. I don't see how I can connect them with the bank mystery. The sneak-thief probably came in wearing a beard, and something went wrong with it. Then he decided to adopt the disguise of a false moustache. It was a clever trick. I wish I could have caught him. I guess I'll get back, and have a talk with Mr. Bentfield."

The bank president was much interested in learning from Larry of the fact of the bricks being so near the place where Witherby boarded.

"It certainly is a clew, Larry, and it might be bad evidence against him, in court," the bank president said. "But, I'm afraid it's too slender to warrant an arrest."

"I think so, too, but I also think that it would be worth while to have Witherby more closely watched than any other of your employees."

"Yes, I agree with you, and I'll order it done. Oh, I do wish this mystery was solved! It isn't so much the money loss, though that is serious enough, as it is that our whole bank system is demoralized by this crime hanging over our heads. Hurry up, Larry, and win that twenty thousand dollars reward!"

"I wish I could, Mr. Bentfield. We'll see what keeping a watch on Witherby brings out."

Close "tabs" were kept on the suspected clerk for several days, but nothing new developed. In the meanwhile Larry had some news in his paper concerning the bank robbery, but it was not much. Some of the other journals, who had put special men on the case, took them off. The detectives were still at work, and several well-known criminals and bank thieves were arrested and put through the "third degree," as it is called by the police, but nothing came of the examinations.

"I don't believe the mystery will ever be solved," said Peter Manton to Larry one day, when both were in police headquarters, after the arrest of a man on suspicion of knowing something of the big case. "I wish my paper would take me off this assignment, and put me on one with more life in it. Don't you want to give up, Larry?"

"I do not! I'm going to solve this."

"You never will," declared Peter. And Larry, as he thought how tangled up the case was now, was not as hopeful as his words indicated.

CHAPTER XIII
THE EXPLOSION

ONE way in which the detectives hoped to get a trace of the man who had the million dollars, provided that it was an employee of the bank who had taken the money, was to note who of the institution's force changed his manner of living.

"For it's a dead-sure thing," said one of the officers, "that whoever stole that money took it to use for himself, or his friends. The only way you can use money is to spend it, and, sooner or later the thief will be spending that money. He'll do it lavishly, too, and then we'll get a line on our man.

"It would be easier, and we could trace him quicker, if we knew the numbers of the bank-notes that were taken. But they don't do things here the way they do in England. There the big bills can be kept track of by their numbers, and many a thief has been caught by that method.

"Of course our money is numbered, but no one ever thinks to make a memoranda of the figures, so that it's almost impossible to trace a stolen note.

"However, there's one thing that's in our favor. Thousand-dollar bills aren't common, and as soon as the thief begins to pass them out he's going to be looked on with suspicion. It may be a long time, but it'll come sooner or later," finished the sleuth.

There was considerable truth in this theory, as Larry well knew. But he made up his mind he could not sit around waiting for the thief to spend some of the money.

"I've got to get quicker action than that," decided the young reporter. "What puzzles me, though, is why the thief hasn't made a move toward getting away before this. If he's still working in the bank, and I'm sure he is, he must be as nervous as a cat for fear some false move will give him away. It's like sleeping over a powder mine, not knowing what minute it may explode. It must be an awful strain."

Then Larry, in his mind, went over all the employees on whom, by any stretch of the imagination, suspicion might fall. He could recall none who acted as though they feared arrest at any moment.

"Whoever he is, he's a star actor, and he ought to go on the stage," decided the young reporter.

The days dragged by. The great bank mystery was all but forgotten by the general public, for other matters filled the newspapers, and it has to be a wonderful piece of news that can keep its place on the front page for more than a week.

Still, Larry managed to get new items from the case every day. If it was not something about his own special assignment to it, he could generally depend on the police to furnish something of interest.

The search for the thief had spread over the whole United States, and to foreign countries as well. But, several weeks after the robbery, there was no more trace of the thief and the missing million dollars than on the first day. It was as if the man and the money had jumped into the sea.

Of course, in a way, a lookout was kept for the man with the beard, who had purchased the valise of Miss Mason, but he was not found. For a time Larry thought to connect him with the sneak-thief at the boarding-house, but he could not do so, and finally concluded that he was wrong on this theory.

From the police of Hackenford, Larry learned that not a thing had been stolen from the boarding-house. Mr. Witherby had returned shortly after Larry left, it was said, and stated that nothing in his room had been disturbed. It was the same with the other lodgers.

"I guess the landlady and I frightened the fellow away before he got a chance to take anything," reasoned Larry, "though from the way he stayed in Witherby's room, juggling with that false beard, it would seem as if he had plenty of spare time."

Larry had not seen Miss Potter since the time he met her in Central Park, with Witherby, though our hero had called on Miss Mason several times. He found in her a most congenial acquaintance. One day, however, when uptown, running down a tip he had received about a foreigner who was spending large sums of money in the hotel district, Larry met the millionaire's daughter.

"Why haven't you been to see me, Larry?" she asked, for during the time her father was missing, and Larry was working on the case, Grace got well acquainted with the young reporter. "Papa said he asked you to call, some time ago, but you never did," she went on.

"Well, I—er—that is, I fancied—" stammered Larry.

"Now I know what you're thinking of!" she exclaimed quickly. "It's Mr. Witherby. Don't deny it!" she went on, playfully shaking a finger at Larry, who was blushing at the correct interpretation of his thoughts. "But I want to tell you," she went on, "that he and I were talking on business matters when you met us."

"Business matters?" repeated Larry.

"Yes. You know Mr. Witherby handles some stocks and bonds down at the bank. Small lots, that borrowers bring in to sell, and which are not important enough to take to a regular broker. Father insists that I shall know something about business, and about investing some money that I have in my own right, and he suggested that Mr. Witherby might give me some advice.

"And he has done so, on several occasions. I have made a number of investments through him, and they have all been good. It was one of these he called to see me about that Sunday, as it was necessary to act early the next morning.

"Besides, he is a distant relative of ours. Most of his people are dead, and he has few friends or relatives. He has ambitions of which he speaks but little. Father wants me to be kind to him and help him all I can.

"It was so pleasant out of doors that I suggested we take a walk. Mr. Witherby is engaged to some girl out West," said Grace, with a laugh which had a meaning of its own. "He showed me her picture. So you see, Larry —"

"I'm sorry I haven't called before," he interrupted, with another blush. "But this bank mystery takes up a lot of time."

"Not so much but what you can go walking in the park with a pretty girl, Larry. Who was she? I'm sure I've seen her before."

Larry explained Miss Mason's position, and then, the little misunderstanding having been cleared away, the two friends walked on down the street together, for Miss Potter had been shopping.

"I have to go away downtown now," she said, after Larry had accompanied her in several stores. "Mamma wants some kind of imported medicine, that I can only get at a wholesale drug house on Greenwich street."

"I'll come along," offered Larry. "I'm about due at the office. That wealthy foreigner clew did not amount to anything." Larry was also wondering what the Witherby clew would amount to, after the remarks of Grace, but he concluded to keep on with it in spite of what she said, for he wanted to clear up the bank mystery.

They were soon riding down in the elevated train, as that was the most convenient way. Talking of many things, and the bank mystery in particular, they hardly noticed the passage of time until the train came to a sudden stop, with a harsh grinding of brakes.

"What's that?" cried Miss Potter.

"Something's happened," exclaimed Larry, his reportorial instinct on the alert at once. "I'll see what it is. You had better sit still."

"No, I want to come with you," she insisted. "I like to know how you reporters work."

"Very well," assented Larry. As they walked toward the end of the car a guard entered.

"What is it?" inquired the young reporter.

"Fire just ahead of us," was the answer. "The flames are shooting up near the track, and we can't get past. We've got to back up to the station we just left."

There was no excitement as yet, and soon the passengers had left the train, and descended to the street to continue their trips in surface cars, or the subway.

"I think I'd better go down to that fire," spoke Larry, with a desire to serve his paper. "It looks like a big one," he added, as he saw clouds of black smoke just ahead. Flames also could be observed, curling above the elevated structure.

"May I come?" asked Miss Potter eagerly. "I won't get in your way, and maybe I can help you."

"Come along," invited our hero, thinking that not every reporter could have a millionaire's daughter for an assistant.

Together they hurried down the street, which was now thronged with an eager crowd rushing toward the fire. Several pieces of the city's fire apparatus were thundering along, the motor engines blowing their sirens like a steamer's foghorn.

"Oh, it's the wholesale drug house where I was going to get mamma's medicine!" cried Miss Potter, when she saw the structure that was ablaze.

"Wait here a minute, until I flash a bulletin to the *Leader*," suggested Larry. "I'll need help if I'm to cover this. I'll be right back."

He rushed to the nearest telephone, and sent in word about the seriousness of the fire, for it was rapidly gaining. He was told to cover it until help arrived, when he would be relieved of the assignment.

"I have a tip on the bank mystery for you," said Mr. Emberg, over the wire. "Get in here as soon as you're relieved."

Larry hurried back to join Miss Potter. He found her eagerly watching the blaze, and the firemen at work.

"Come," said Larry, "we'll get a little closer."

His reporter's badge admitted him inside the fire lines, and a word to a policeman, whom Larry knew, made it easy for Miss Potter to accompany him. She was fascinated by this near view of a big conflagration.

Larry was busy getting facts about how the blaze had started, and he had jotted down a note about a sensational rescue of a woman clerk by one of the firemen, when a man rushed along the press of people, crying:

"Back! Get back, everybody! The fire has eaten down into the basement, where a lot of oils and chemicals are stored! There'll be an explosion in another minute! Get back!"

Police and firemen took up the cry, and began shoving the crowds out of danger. Larry and Miss Potter moved to a place of safety.

Hardly had this been done than there came a sharp explosion from the big drug house. It slightly shook the ground.

"That's only the first! There'll be more!" cried the man who had given the alarm. "Get farther back!"

"We'd better get out of danger!" shouted Larry in the girl's ear, for the noise was such that ordinary tones could not be heard. "Come on!"

He took her arm to help her through the crowd. As he did so there came a terrific explosion, and the glass in many buildings nearby was shattered.

"This is fierce!" yelled Larry. "It's going to make a big newspaper story! We haven't had a large fire in a long time."

CHAPTER XIV
PLANNING A SEARCH

FEARING that the next explosion might be even worse, and not only shatter the glass, but throw down some of the surrounding buildings themselves, Larry fairly pulled Miss Potter out of danger.

As he rushed along, surrounded on all sides by a frantic, pushing, shouting mob, the young reporter happened to glance up at one of the structures, the windows of which had nearly all been destroyed by the blast. One floor of this building was occupied by a costumer, who, as an advertisement, had set a figure of a clown, in an odd costume, on the sill of one casement. The explosion had turned this clown upside down.

As Larry was speculating on this odd sight, and making a mental note of it, to be used in the story, his attention was attracted by something else. Owing to the breaking of the glass of the costumer's windows, many of which were of ground, or painted material, so that the public could not observe his customers trying on suits, a full view could be had into the interior of the shop.

Hung up all around were costumes of various ages, and of characters from knights and harlequins, to monks and fairy dancers.

But none of these attracted Larry just then, for with startling suddenness he beheld, in the middle of one room, a man standing, a man whom the young reporter knew at once to be Witherby, the bank clerk!

And Witherby held in his hand a black moustache—a false moustache —as if, at the time of the explosion, he had been about to adjust it, but had been startled by the blowing out of the windows.

"By Jove!" ejaculated Larry.

"What—what is it? Some one hurt?" gasped Miss Potter, at his side.

"No, but—"

Larry hesitated, and had made up his mind he would not call the attention of the millionaire's daughter to the strange sight. But it was too late. She had seen Witherby, and had caught sight of the false moustache in his hand.

"Oh! Oh!" she gasped. "What—what does that mean, Larry?"

Before he could answer there came another explosion, and hoarse shouts of fear and warning.

"This is getting too much for me!" thought Larry. "I'm between two fires. I've just got to get after this new clew to the bank mystery, and yet I can't leave this fire and explosion uncovered. What shall I do? I wonder what game Witherby is up to now? I'll wager he's getting ready to skip out with the million dollars! I must get word to Mr. Bentfield at once. I guess it's time to cause an arrest!

"But what about this fire? I've got to stay on this until some of the *Leader* boys come. Why don't they hurry?"

"Can I help you?" asked Miss Potter, seeing what was in Larry's mind.

"Yes, you might," he said. "I want to stay here, where I can—well, where I can keep my eye on a certain person," he corrected himself quickly. "And yet I want to get word to the office, asking the boys to hurry here."

"I can telephone for you," she offered, and she was just going to do that when a young man rushed up to Larry. He was a fellow reporter.

"I'm sent to relieve you," he said. "The boss wants you back in the office as soon as you can get there. What's happened so far?"

Rapidly Larry told the main facts of the fire and explosion, and gave all the helpful points he could to his fellow scribe. By this time several other of the *Leader* men had arrived on the scene, as well as representatives from other papers.

"I'll give 'em all I have, and you can take up the story from now on," suggested Larry to his friends. "I guess some were hurt in that blow-up. Look out for more to follow."

He hurried off to the nearest telephone, with Miss Potter, and soon had sent in over the wire all the news he had. He also flashed something about having seen Witherby, as if disguising himself for flight. Larry was sure the bank clerk had not observed him, because of the excitement over the explosions.

"If he did see me he may take the alarm, and light out ahead of time," thought the young reporter. "I've got to get busy. Guess I'll go back to the costumer's and see what I can learn there before I go to the office."

First, however, after pledging her to silence, he put Miss Potter on a car to go to her home. She had had enough of the excitement, she said. Then Larry hurried back to the scene of the fire. The drug house was still burning fiercely, and it proved to be one of the worst blazes New York ever had experienced.

Because of the damage to his windows, and the fear of what might follow, the costumer could give Larry little information, that amounted to anything, about Witherby.

"I don't know the man you speak of," said the costumer to the reporter. "Many people come in here every day to buy false wigs, beards or moustaches for themselves. I do not ask their names. They may want them for theatricals, or for criminal disguises. I have no way of telling. A number were in here when the explosion blew out all my windows. Oh, it was terrible! I am all upset. I don't know the young man you speak of. At any rate, he is gone—they are all gone who were in here. The explosion scared them. Oh, so much as I will lose by this! Some of my best costumes are spoiled!"

This was true, for dirt and dust had sifted in the opened windows after the explosion, and now black smoke was entering in dense clouds.

Even as Larry was talking there came a series of light explosions, and, fearing there might be more, and severer ones, the police ordered every one out of the buildings near the burning structure.

"I guess it's time for me to go," thought Larry. "I can't learn anything more here, and I want to get on Witherby's trail. He's certainly up to something. It's a good thing he has an outside job, or he couldn't be away from the bank so much to make his plans. But I think I've got him pat now. If only I'm not too late!"

As Larry hurried from the costumer's there came an explosion worse than any of the preceding ones. He wanted to stay, and help cover the story, which he knew would be a big one, but a reporter, like a soldier, has to obey orders, and Mr. Emberg had sent for him to come in.

"I wonder what his tip is, about the bank mystery?" thought Larry, as he hurried on to the *Leader* office. "I don't believe it is as good as mine."

That Mr. Emberg was surprised when Larry gave all the details of seeing Witherby with the false moustache is to put it mildly.

"It's going to be a great yarn, Larry!" exclaimed the city editor. "Keep right after it. This is my tip. One of the headquarters' detectives is on the trail of one of the bank directors, I understand."

"He is?" cried Larry. "Then I think I know which one."

"Who is it?"

"Mr. Wilson. He and Witherby are quite chummy. Say, wouldn't it be great, if it should turn out that he and Witherby pulled off this robbery together?"

"And are going to escape together with the million dollars," added Mr. Emberg, his eyes sparkling in anticipation of the sensational story that would develop.

"I'll get right after it," exclaimed Larry, and then the thought came to him that Mr. Wilson might have been the man with the beard who had bought the valise.

"I'll have to arrange for Miss Mason to see him," he thought. "She may be able to identify him."

His first visit was to the detective whom the city editor had mentioned as having a clew to the bank director.

"It wouldn't be the first time a bank official has robbed his own institution," thought Larry. "And Wilson certainly acted very queer about this case."

When he saw the detective, however, he found that the clew was so slender as to be hardly worth following. Still, the young reporter knew that he must neglect nothing.

"The first thing to be done is to search Witherby's room," declared Larry, in talking to the bank president of the latest development. "He may have the money concealed there. And we've got to act quickly or he may escape. Can you arrange it?"

"I think so. I expect him in soon, and when he does come I'll give him something to do that will keep him out of town over-night. Then, with the proper police authority, which I can arrange for, we'll search his room. His buying a false moustache certainly looks suspicious, Larry. But I don't take any stock in this about Mr. Wilson."

"Nor I," agreed the reporter. "But may I help in the search of Witherby's room?"

"Certainly. I intend that you shall be there. I'll call my lawyer now, and arrange for the proper authority."

CHAPTER XV
THE THOUSAND-DOLLAR BILL

HARRISON WITHERBY showed no surprise when, a little later that afternoon, a messenger summoned him to the private office of the bank president. But if he was calm and collected over it, the other clerks and employees were not.

"Say, I'll wager something is up," whispered one of the bookkeepers to another.

"Shouldn't wonder," was the answer. "About the robbery, too."

"That's right! It's a shame it hasn't been solved before, so that every one isn't under suspicion."

"It sure is, but I don't see how Witherby could have taken the valise. He had no chance."

"There's no telling. I thought that reporter fellow on the *Leader* was going to solve this thing in jig style, but I guess he isn't any better than any one else."

"That's so. Well, I wonder what Witherby is in for?"

The suspected bank clerk showed no surprise when given the assignment that would take him out of town over-night. He had often gone on such errands before, and if, on this occasion, it interfered with his plans, he did not betray that fact.

"I want you to see this bank president," said Mr. Bentfield, naming one who was the head of an institution some distance from New York, in a small country town. "Tell him I have agreed to his proposition about that loan, and about acting as his correspondent for the Metropolitan section. I'll give you the papers for him to sign."

"Very well, Mr. Bentfield. I'll start to-night, as soon as I can go out to my boarding place."

"No, I don't believe you have time for that," said the bank president quickly, for Larry had suggested this possibility: that, if Witherby was sent out of town, he would not come back; and if he had the million dollars hidden at his boarding place he would take the cash away with him. He must not be allowed, therefore, to go to his room until after the search.

"There is a train leaving the Grand Central station in a few minutes," said Mr. Bentfield. "You can catch it by taking a taxicab. Here is money for your expenses, in case you need it, and if you want a change of clothing buy it, and put it on your expense bill. I want you to see this bank official to-night, if possible. I'll telegraph him that you are coming, but you would miss him if you took a later train, and you'd have to, if you went out to your boarding-house."

"Very well," assented the bank clerk, and his manner was not at all disturbed, as he took the cash for his expenses.

"Well, if he had anything to do with the robbery of the million dollars he's the coolest person I ever had any dealings with," thought Mr. Bentfield. "He certainly is a good actor. But though I hope we find out who the guilty one is, and get the money back, I should dislike to learn that it was Witherby. Certainly he has his faults, but I think he is a good young man—or he was before he was tempted and fell—if he did."

A little later Larry reached the bank again, and was closeted with the president.

"Well, I've got Witherby out of the way," Mr. Bentfield remarked. "Now to make the search. Did you succeed in getting the warrant giving us permission to look through his room?" he asked of the lawyer, who was also present.

"I had to arrange for it by telephone. It will be waiting for us in Hackenford. It is going to be rather a delicate piece of work, Mr. Bentfield. It is sure to arouse suspicion in the mind of Mr. Witherby as soon as he learns of it."

"I'll fix it so he won't know of it," exclaimed Larry.

"How?" inquired the lawyer.

"Well, as soon as I have the necessary legal permission, I'll go to Mrs. Boland, the landlady, and tell her what I propose doing. I'll tell her it is necessary, for the reputation of her house, that it be kept quiet, and that, when Witherby returns, he shall not even get a hint that his room has been entered."

"But he'll see his things disturbed," suggested the bank president.

"I intend to do the searching all by myself," said Larry. "I'll put everything back where I find it."

"But the other boarders in the house," came from the lawyer. "They will surely suspect something."

"Not if I can get Mrs. Boland to help me. I'll see her alone, explain what I want, and suggest that I'd like to see our suspect and that I be allowed to wait for Witherby in his room. I can pretend to be a sort of acquaintance, who wants to see him, you know. Then I can make my search and get away. If I find nothing suspicious, that will end it. If I get a clew, then—"

"An arrest will follow!" exclaimed Mr. Bentfield. "Justice must be done, no matter what the result. The bank owes it to itself, and the other clerks, who are under an unjust suspicion, must be cleared, Larry, the quicker this is over with the better."

The young reporter lost no time in starting for Hackenford. He planned to reach it before the other boarders came home to supper, as that would make his task easier. The lawyer went with him to secure the search-warrant, and then returned to New York.

Mrs. Boland, the landlady, was much surprised to see again the young man who had been present on the other sensational occasion, when the sneak-thief was discovered.

"Did you come back about a room?" she asked Larry.

"Not exactly," he said. "I must see you in private," he added, as he saw a servant standing in the dining-room.

"Is anything wrong—has anything happened?" asked the boarding mistress when they were alone. Larry briefly told her of the suspicions against Witherby, and his desire to search his room, at the same time showing the necessary authority.

"Oh, to think of that!" cried Mrs. Boland. "A million dollars in my house!"

"It may not be here," suggested Larry, with a smile. "I hope it is, but I have my doubts. Still, I may get a clew. I must ask you to be silent about my visit here."

Overawed by the search-warrant and the magnitude of the case, the landlady readily promised to say nothing to a soul. She would also keep from Witherby, on his return, the fact that his room had been entered.

"I'll go up to it now, before any of the other lodgers come home," suggested Larry, and he was shown to the apartment which might hold the solution of the mystery.

Mrs. Boland left the young reporter alone. Larry went at his work systematically. He had often been with the police, or detectives, when they searched the rooms of other suspected persons, and he knew pretty well how to proceed.

For an hour or more Larry went over everything, looking in bureau and desk drawers, in the trunk, under the carpet—in fact, in any place where money might be concealed.

"It can't be in any small place," argued Larry, "for the bundles of bills are rather bulky. Still, he may have divided them, and hidden a few each in many places."

He renewed his search, being careful to keep the room in the same order as he found it, but he was unsuccessful. He was about to give up, regretfully, and he had already begun to formulate new clews in his mind, when from the bottom of a bureau drawer he picked up a small book. At the sight of it Larry started, for it was a book, or catalogue, from a concern dealing in false beards, wigs and other theatrical disguises.

"This is where he got his ideas of false moustaches from," thought Larry. Idly he leafed the book. Something fluttered from between two pages to the floor.

The young reporter stooped to pick it up, and he could hardly believe the evidence of his own eyes when he saw, lying on the floor, a thousand-dollar bill!

"Great Scott!" whispered Larry. "It's real!"

He fingered it, thinking for the moment that it might be "stage money." But his touch told him that it was genuine.

"What have I found? What have I found?" he murmured. "The stolen million was all in thousand-dollar bills! Is this the only one left?"

As he stood in the middle of the floor, holding the bill in his fingers, there was a step in the hall outside.

CHAPTER XVI
A STRANGE DISCOVERY

"Who's that?" thought Larry instantly. "If it's Witherby he'll take the alarm, and go at once. But no, it can't be that chap. He's too far off. And if it's any of the other boarders he won't come in—that is, unless he's a friend of Witherby's, who may walk in unawares. If he sees this—"

Larry looked down at the thousand-dollar bill he held, and then he glanced at the door. With noiseless steps he crossed the room, and was about to turn the key in the lock, a precaution he felt he should have taken before, when there came a tap on the portal.

"It's a stranger, or some of the other boarders," thought Larry. "Mrs. Boland would walk right in. What shall I do?"

As he stood there irresolutely, holding the incriminating bit of evidence between his fingers, Larry heard a voice in an unmistakable foreign accent ask:

"Are yez in there, Mr. Witherby?"

"A woman!" thought Larry. "One of the maids, evidently."

"Becaze av yez are in there, Mr. Witherby, th' missus sint me some time ago t' mek th' room up, an' I clane forgot it. So I'll be after doin' it now, av yez ain't in it. Be yez there, Mr. Witherby?"

What answer should Larry make? The girl, unsuspecting though she might be, would be likely to know Witherby's voice, and raise an alarm if she heard a strange one. Nor was Larry confident of his ability to make his tones sound like those of the absent boarder. He was puzzled as to what to do. If only Mrs. Boland had remained on guard, she could have sent the servant away. But the landlady had probably gone downstairs.

"Are yez there, Mr. Witherby?" came the voice again. "Becaze I must do that room or th' missus'll be displazed, an' me only after gittin' th' job here t'day. 'Clane Mr. Witherby's room,' sez th' missus t' me this marnin, an' I clane forgot it until now. But av yez are out, Mr. Witherby, I'll do it now."

Larry had an inspiration.

"A new servant!" he reflected. "She probably has never seen Witherby, and doesn't know his voice. I'm safe."

So he made answer.

"I'm in here now, Bridget, and you can't clean the room."

"Sure, how did you know my name was Bridget, which it ain't, bein' Katie. But, av it's all th' same t' yez, ye'll have t' step out while I do th' room. Come now, Mr. Witherby, come out like a gintleman, an' let me in."

"No, Katie, I can't," and Larry smiled at the strange order.

"Yez'll have t'! Didn't th' missus tell me t' clane th' room? Come out now, like a gintleman, or I'll lose me place."

"No, Katie," said Larry. "Do some other room, and I'll soon be out. I'll explain to Mrs. Boland."

"Will yez? Thin it'll be all right, glory be!" and the servant passed on down the hall, much to Larry's relief.

"That was a close shave," he reflected. "I must get through here, or I won't be so lucky next time. To think that I found the thousand-dollar bill—and the stolen million was in bills of this denomination! Oh, if they only had the numbers of some of them!"

Larry made a note of the bill he held in his hand, and then, slipping it back between the pages of the theatrical book, he placed the latter where he had found it. He made a cursory search through a drawer he had overlooked, not expecting to find anything, but what was his surprise to find in it a false, sandy moustache! A wave of memory swept over him.

"Great Scott!" he whispered. "Now I understand! Witherby has several disguises. It was he who was in this room, trying on the black beard the day I discovered the bricks in the new house. He was the man we thought was the sneak-thief! He walked out of his own room, with this false moustache on, and neither Mrs. Boland nor I recognized him. He fooled us both. And we thought him a sneak-thief!"

Larry could not but help admiring the nerve of the suspected bank clerk.

"I wonder why he did it?" reflected Larry. "I have it! He heard us talking, he had seen me spying on him. He reasoned that the game was up, and by a colossal piece of bluff, he walked out of his room, right under my nose, and took most of the million dollars with him. He left this thousand-dollar bill to provide money for his escape. He's got the million salted away, and he may skip out any minute, and get to it. Then—good-night!"

Larry thought rapidly. Certainly quick action was necessary. He put the false moustache back in the drawer, gave a hurried glance about the room, to make sure the clerk, on his return, would notice nothing awry, and then went downstairs. He found Mrs. Boland waiting for him.

"Well?" she asked anxiously.

"I think I had better say nothing," answered Larry. "If you know nothing you will not worry."

"Oh, but did you find anything? Is Mr. Witherby—?"

"I had rather not answer," spoke Larry. "When Mr. Witherby comes back please say nothing to him. There may be big developments in the next few hours."

"Oh, but to think of the disgrace that may come to my boarding-house!" she cried.

"I think I can promise you that there will be no shadow of disgrace," said Larry. "By the way, your new servant wanted to get in to clean his room, while I was there. I put her off. You had best explain to her."

"Oh, yes, you mean Katie. I will. I forgot about her when I let you go up. Oh, but I hope there will be nothing disgraceful, for I have always kept a respectful place, Mr. Dexter."

"Don't worry," said Larry kindly, for he felt sorry for the landlady.

As he was on his way back to New York, Larry thought of many things. Clearly something must be done at once. He must see Mr. Bentfield. Probably the banker would order the clerk's arrest, when he learned of the false moustache, and the thousand-dollar bill.

"And I'll get a great story!" thought the young reporter. "I'm sorry for the poor fellow, though. Maybe the temptation was more than he could stand. A million dollars is a lot of money."

On reaching New York, Larry called Mr. Bentfield up on the telephone, giving a hint of the disclosure he had to make.

"I'd like to have a talk with you, Mr. Bentfield," said Larry, over the wire. "Shall I call at your house?"

"No, I had rather meet you at the bank. I know it's rather late, but we can be undisturbed there. I'll have my lawyer with me, and, if necessary to act, we can do so from there. Besides, Witherby won't be back until morning. I'll telephone the watchman at the bank to admit you. Go in, and make yourself comfortable. I'll be down as soon as I can."

"All right," answered Larry, and he started for the bank in Wall street.

CHAPTER XVII
BEHIND THE OLD BOOKS

"Now, Larry, tell us all about it," invited Mr. Bentfield a little later, when, with his lawyer, he had greeted the young reporter in his private office of the bank. It was past midnight, and, had any one looked into that room, he might have wondered what brought the three there, to hold a secret conference.

"Well, I made two strange discoveries," Larry answered. "I think, Mr. Bentfield, that we are about at the end of the trail. I can't promise you the million dollars, but I believe I can name the thief. He's the one I have suspected from the first. Now for my evidence."

Larry quickly went over all his work on the bank mystery case from the beginning. Then he gave more details of his location of the tell-tale bricks, so near Witherby's boarding place, telling of seeing the man at the window, trying on the false beard.

"And now comes the climax," went on Larry, as he told of finding the thousand-dollar bill, and the false, sandy moustache.

"By Jove!" exclaimed the lawyer, "I never would have believed it! Of course, he's the guilty one, Bentfield. You should notify the police, and have him arrested at once. In fact, I think I would not wait for his return. He may never come back. Send word out to this place, where he has gone on business for you, and have him taken into custody there. Get him out of bed if necessary. He may have the million with him."

"Poor fellow!" said the bank president softly. "It is sad to think of it. I am just beginning to realize how hard it must be for a bank clerk, on a comparatively small salary, to see millions of dollars every day, and know that he must not touch them. And most of them are young fellows, with a love for the pleasures of life. It is hard, very hard! A great temptation!"

"Stuff and nonsense!" exclaimed the lawyer gruffly. "They should resist temptation. The money is not theirs. If they take it they must suffer the consequences. Call up the police at once, and have them arrest this fellow. I congratulate you, young man," he said to Larry. "You have worked up a difficult case in a masterly manner. I congratulate you. Yes, hum!"

"It isn't finished yet," said Larry, who had seen many a good story go to pieces at the last minute. "Wait until we get the thief, and the million."

"Oh, we as good as have the thief, but I can't say so much for the money," spoke the lawyer, confidently.

"All I ask," said Larry, "is that you will see that I get the first information on this case. I want the story exclusively. That is why I have worked so hard on it—to get a 'beat' for the *Leader*."

"You shall have it, you shall have it," said the bank president slowly. "Poor fellow! Poor Witherby! I suppose there is no other way than to have him arrested?" He looked at the legal gentleman anxiously.

"A way out? Of course not, my dear sir. He must be arrested. Call up the police at once."

"I suppose I'll have to," sighed Mr. Bentfield. "And yet I had great hopes of that young man. He had a hasty temper, but he was getting control of it. Too bad—too bad."

He reached for the telephone on his desk, but Larry stayed his hand.

"One moment, Mr. Bentfield," said the young reporter. "I think, now that this case seems likely to come to an issue, that we had better be sure of our ground."

"What do you mean?"

"I mean that, in all likelihood, Witherby will deny that he took the money."

"But we can prove that he had part of it in his possession!" exclaimed the lawyer testily.

"I'm afraid not," went on Larry. "Thousand-dollar bills are not so very uncommon. No one knows the numbers of the stolen ones, it seems. And, it has been my experience, that no matter how good the evidence, or how complete the case against a criminal, he will deny it, in the hope of puzzling a jury."

And as Larry spoke thus he could not help thinking of how it might affect Grace Potter—to know that her friend and distant relative was a bank thief. Larry almost wished he did not have to solve the mystery.

"Well, I suppose you are right," admitted the lawyer. "I have had very little practice in criminal cases."

"What do you suggest, Larry?" asked the banker.

"I think that we should go carefully over the ground, and see if there are any weak points," replied the young reporter. "If we have to resort to circumstantial evidence we ought to be able to show, step by step, how the chain of evidence is made up. In the first place, would it have been possible for Witherby to have gotten to the bag that morning, after the million dollars was put in it?"

"I think it would," answered the president. "Suppose we go out into the main room, and look over the ground? It may help us on the case."

The three went out into the dimly lighted "cage" where, during business hours, so much money changed hands.

"Here is where the bank-notes were put into the bag," said Mr. Bentfield, pointing to a low desk. "I know, because I was present at the time. It was one of the biggest transactions we ever undertook, and I wanted no mistakes. I saw the bundles of notes put into the steel-mesh-lined bag. It was then locked, and set close to the chief cashier's desk, on the floor. There were a number of clerks and tellers all around, and it would have been impossible for a stranger—an outsider—to have come in the cage. We can easily prove that, if Witherby sets up, as a defense, that some one other than a bank employee might have committed the theft."

"After the bag was placed on the floor, what happened?" asked Larry, who wanted to refresh his memory.

"It stayed there until it was picked up, to be taken to the other bank. Then the theft was discovered, as you know."

Larry looked around the cage. It was like most banks. In front of the brass grill work, and inside of it, was a long desk, at about the height of a man's chest. It was at this desk that the various tellers and bookkeepers worked, and took in the money from depositors, or paid it out through little wickets.

On the other side of the cage was a similar long desk, at which several bookkeepers could work on the sloping top. This desk was not used by the public at all, but at it the bank's books were made up, money counted and put into packages, and similar things done. Underneath this desk were several closets, or compartments, closed by sliding doors.

"What are they for?" asked Larry, pointing to the closets.

"Oh, unimportant books are kept in them, and some of the clerks use them to put their rubbers or umbrellas in. Nothing of any account," and Mr. Bentfield opened several of the doors. Many of the compartments were empty, and in one was a small valise.

"Whose is that?" asked Larry.

"Oh, it belongs to some of the clerks, I suppose," answered the president. "Often they go out of town for week-end visits. To save time so as not to have to go back home, or to their boarding-places, after the bank closes, they bring their valises down here with their change of clothes in, and take the train from here. That is nothing."

"No," agreed Larry. His gaze went farther about the cage and rested on the open door of a sort of closet, or vault. It was practically a vault, for there was a heavy iron portal to it.

"Is that where you keep the bank's money, Mr. Bentfield?" Larry asked, with a smile. "It does not seem to be a very safe place."

"No, that's a vault where we keep old ledgers that are out of use. We file them away merely for reference. They are seldom looked at, and sometimes we burn them up. The vault is fire-proof, and that's the most that can be said of it. I don't know why the door wasn't closed to-night. Some one was careless."

Hardly knowing why he did it, Larry walked into this vault. There was an incandescent lamp swinging from the ceiling by a green cord. The young reporter reached up, and switched it on. He still had no particular object in his actions. It was more to cover every bit of the ground, so as to be in a position to testify accurately, in case he was called on as a witness, as would be probable.

There were rows and rows of old ledgers on the shelves of the vault. Big, heavy books, some of them nearly a foot thick. Their gold-lettered backs stood out in the glow of the electric light.

"I shouldn't want to carry many of those books around," said Larry, as he raised his hand to push against one of the largest, and so judge of its weight. "They are pretty heavy. I should think—"

But he never finished that sentence. For, as his fingers came in contact with the back of the old ledger it moved—it slid in on the shelf, and, not only did that book move, but also the one next to it. And Larry knew, full well, that not by a mere pressure of his fingers could he move one of the heavy books on the shelf, to say nothing of two.

"What is it? What is the matter?" demanded Mr. Bentfield, attracted by something strange in the young reporter's action. "Have you found anything of importance?"

Larry did not answer. He tried to push a book that stood next to the two which he had been able to move with such ease. He found it impossible.

Only by exerting considerable strength was he able to slide the other old ledger back. But it was different in the case of the first two. They moved at a touch. There could be but one reason. They were dummies!

As this thought flashed into Larry's mind he reached up and, taking hold of the tops of the light ledgers, he pulled them toward him. They came away amid a cloud of dust, leaving a gaping space in the row of books.

And then something tumbled from the place they had occupied. A bag —a leather bag, which rolled over and over on the floor of the vault to the very feet of the president. The leather backs of the old ledgers had been glued to the bag, and, when Larry pulled, they came out from the row of books, bringing the bag with them. But the glue had not held well, and the weight of the bag, once it was off the shelf, had pulled it loose.

There it lay, on the floor, and Larry stood holding the backs of the ledgers, from which the covers and pages had been cut with a sharp knife. But it was the bag on which all eyes rested.

"It's the bank's bag! The bag that held the million dollars!" cried the president, leaning over to grasp it. "It's the bag for which the dummy one was exchanged! What an amazing discovery!"

"See if the million is in it!" hoarsely suggested Larry.

CHAPTER XVIII
WITHERBY VANISHES

FOR a moment it seemed as if no one knew what to do. All stood there looking at the bag that had so suddenly, and so mysteriously, appeared.

"I—I'm actually afraid to open it," whispered Mr. Bentfield. "Suppose —suppose the money shouldn't be there?"

"Very likely it isn't," commented the lawyer dryly.

This seemed to galvanize the bank president into action. Quickly he lifted up the valise, and, as he did so, a change came over his face. It had been hopeful, now it showed despair.

"The money is gone!" he gasped.

"How do you know?" asked the lawyer sharply.

"The bag is too light-weighted to contain a million, or a large part of it. See!"

He quickly opened the valise. It was not locked. One look inside showed that it contained nothing. The thief had taken away the bundles of bills.

"Are you sure that is the same valise in which the million was originally packed?" asked Larry. "The one lined with the steel mesh?"

"It's lined with steel, all right," answered the banker, "and while I could not swear that this is the bank's bag, I am morally certain it is. Some of the tellers can prove that. But that will be of little value in court. The fact that the money is gone is of more importance.

"My, my! But this mystery grows instead of solving itself," he went on. "To think of finding the bag back of the old ledgers! The plot was well thought out. How did you come to lift down those books, Larry?"

"It was impulse, at first, that led me to put my hand on them, and when I found that they were so light, and could be shoved along so easily, I was suspicious at once."

"And with good cause," added the lawyer. "But I can't quite see how the trick was worked."

"Nor I," admitted Larry. "It is certain, however, that after the exchange of the bags, the thief brought the one containing the million in here. Just how soon after the theft can only be guessed at. Then he cut off the backs of the ledgers, pasted them on the narrow end of the valise, shoved it in the space the books occupied, and it was as well hidden as if he had buried it."

"Better," commented Mr. Bentfield, "for, if he had buried the money, the ground would have been disturbed, and some one would have been suspicious. As it was, no one would ever think of looking behind these old books. Sometimes several years go by without any one referring to them. It was a safe place to hide a million dollars, and yet it was right in the bank!"

"Do you think the million was ever actually there?" asked the lawyer.

"Perhaps not," admitted Larry. "The thief, after he switched, or changed, the bags, may have watched his chance, that very night, to take away the money. Then, to get rid of the empty valise, he may have put it behind the old ledgers. But he must have planned to do that, otherwise he would not have had the backs cut away. And he had to have glue to stick them on the valise. All that indicates the fact of preparation."

"Well, the money is gone, that's certain," spoke the lawyer dryly. "And the next thing to consider is, how to arrest the thief, and get it back. I don't suppose you now have any scruples about giving Witherby into custody, Mr. Bentfield?"

"No, and yet I can't see how the finding of the empty bag proves anything more against him. I think he is guilty, but the latest development does not add anything to it."

"That's right," admitted Larry. "But it will make a good story for me."

"Oh, you newspaper reporters!" exclaimed the lawyer. "All you think of is to get good newspaper stories."

"That's our profession," answered Larry, with a smile. And yet he could not help but think of Grace Potter—of the unpleasantness that might annoy her.

"You had better call up the police at once," suggested the lawyer to the bank president, and Mr. Bentfield agreed. Soon he was in communication with the authorities.

Though it was past midnight, he managed to get on the wire the detective department in the town where Witherby had gone on the bank's business. Mr. Bentfield received the promise that the arrest would be made at once, and he would be notified as soon as this took place.

"Then we'll wait here until we get that word," said the president. "We can make ourselves comfortable in my private office, and see what the telephone says."

They waited, talking at intervals about the strange case. Larry thought over the points of the story he would write the next day. The finding of the valise, so strangely hidden, would make sensational reading.

Suddenly there came the tinkle of the telephone bell. Mr. Bentfield reached for the instrument.

"Yes—yes, this is the Consolidated National," he answered. "Yes, I'm the president. What's that? You went to arrest Witherby, at the hotel where he was stopping over-night. Yes—yes! Well, go on, hurry up. Did you get him?"

"What? You didn't? Why not?"

"He'd gone! What's that? Do I get you right? He'd gone? Taken an early morning train for New York? My, that's strange!"

Mr. Bentfield placed his hand over the transmitter of the telephone, and, turning to Larry and the lawyer, said:

"He's gone! Left for New York. They can't arrest him there."

"All right," said the lawyer, who thought quickly. "Tell them we'll look after the case from this end. Ring off, and get police headquarters here. Give them a description of Witherby, and tell them to watch his boarding place in Hackenford, or have the police there do it. It would be better to have a New York detective on the case. We'll nab him when he comes to get his thousand-dollar bill."

This request was soon sent over the wire, and word came back that a man would be detailed to watch the boarding place of the suspected man.

"And that's all we can do now," said the lawyer. "Let's go home."

Larry paid an early visit to the bank the next morning. He was at once admitted to Mr. Bentfield's room.

"Have you heard anything from Hackenford?" asked the reporter.

In reply, the bank president handed him a telegram. It read:

"House carefully watched. Man described did not enter or
leave it."

"He seems to have disappeared," remarked the president. "What do you think of it, Larry?"

"I don't know what to think. But I'm going out to Hackenford, and see the man who was watching the house. There's something wrong somewhere."

CHAPTER XIX
LARRY ON THE TRAIL

THOSE were busy days for Larry Dexter. Not only did he have to consider his paper, and arrange for a story each day about the bank mystery, but he had to act as a sort of detective, and keep after the various ends of the puzzling case. No wonder that he was not home much, and that his mother complained that she was forgetting what he looked like.

For the *Leader* wanted something each day about the big story. Very frequently a newspaper will begin a "crusade," or take up some special line, and the reporter assigned to it has to turn in so much "copy" a day, no matter whether there is any news or not.

No sooner had the young reporter heard, from the bank president, that the suspected clerk had disappeared, than he arranged to go to Hackenford.

"There's where the main news is now," thought Larry. "There must be some reason why Witherby did not come back. He must suspect something. Maybe he's skipped out with the million, and doesn't miss the thousand-dollar bill he left behind. I've got to get after him, no matter where he's gone."

The young reporter prepared his story of the finding of the bag, so cunningly hidden behind the old ledgers. Then, after a talk with Mr. Emberg, he left for Hackenford.

"See what you can pick up there, Larry," suggested the city editor. "If you think it will spoil the case to write anything about it, don't do it. What we want you to do is to find the thief and the million, and there won't be any doubt but what you'll get a 'beat' out of it."

Arriving in Hackenford, Larry at once sought out the detective who had been sent to watch the boarding-house where Witherby had his room. Larry had been told where to look for the official.

The latter, who was a good man in his own line, which was getting evidence against counterfeiters, was all at sea when it came to spying on a person such as the reporter believed Harrison Witherby to be. The detective had engaged a room across the street from the boarding-house, giving it out that he was a photographer, looking for new subjects.

To carry out this idea he had improvised a shelf on the window ledge of his room, and was making blue prints of nothing in particular when Larry found him, for the detective had not given up the case, though it looked hopeless.

"Well?" asked the young reporter.

"No, bad," replied the detective, shortly. "I've kept a careful watch of that place over there, and I'm sure your man hasn't come in or out. I've been at the window nearly all the while from early this morning, before daylight, when I got here, until now, and nobody, at all resembling the person you spoke of, has shown up."

"How about back doors?" asked Larry.

"I've got a man with me. He's guarding the back. He hasn't seen any one, either."

"You don't mean to tell me that no one has gone in or out of that boarding-house since before breakfast this morning?" asked Larry, in surprise.

"Of course not," replied the detective. "A lot of people came out, and some went in. I've got descriptions of all of 'em, but none fit. Here, I'll read 'em to you," and he proceeded to do so. There were women and men who had gone in, or come out, but no one tallied with the description of Witherby. The only person to enter the back door was a milkman, and Larry at once dismissed him from consideration.

"Well, I guess he didn't come back here then," the young reporter remarked, referring to Witherby. "He must have gotten suspicious and left. I think I'll try and get up to his room again."

"Think there may be more clews there?" asked the representative of the law.

"There might be. Let's see, you've got a note here of a man with a long, white beard entering the boarding-house."

"Yes, he went in early this morning, soon after I got here. It was shortly after breakfast, and the woman here was quite surprised to get one as a boarder so early. I told her I wanted to get some photographs of the sunrise, and she thought that was all right. The white-bearded man entered, and he hasn't come out yet, so he must be there."

"And no one has come out who looks like Witherby?"

"Not a soul. I've been right on the job."

Larry hardly knew what to do. It seemed that the bank clerk was not in his boarding-house, and yet the young reporter had learned not to trust to appearances.

"I think I'll just go over and take a look, and make some inquiries," he decided. "You had better stay around here. You may get some clew when you least expect it."

"All right!" agreed the detective, "though I think your man has skipped out, and never came near this place."

Larry shrugged his shoulders. He did not know what to think. A few minutes later he was talking to Mrs. Boland.

"A man with a white beard!" she exclaimed when the young reporter had asked if she had such a boarder. "Why, there's no one like that in this house! You must be mistaken."

But Larry knew he was not. He also knew what to expect.

"I see," he reasoned. "Witherby came back here, disguised as an old man. That's why the detective didn't know him. And he probably went out disguised like a baker, or a butcher, and so he got away. He fooled the detective all right, and he's fooled me. I've got to get after him."

He thought rapidly for a few minutes.

"May I go to Mr. Witherby's room again?" he asked of the landlady. She gave him permission.

But it was quite a different room to which the young reporter gained entrance a little later. All the bank clerk's possessions had been taken away. The thousand-dollar bill was gone, and so was the false, sandy moustache.

"He's skipped all right," mused Larry. "He came in here while it was dark this morning, and sneaked his things out. Then he left himself. Now it's going to be a job to find him."

"He had his board all paid up," said the landlady.

"A pity he wouldn't, with a million dollars," thought Larry.

Once more his brain worked rapidly.

"If this thing comes out," he reasoned, "all the other papers will jump to the conclusion that Witherby is the thief. They'll have stories about him. I've got to keep this quiet until I find him, and clinch things. I'll have to arrange with Mr. Bentfield for secrecy."

He did so, planning to have it generally understood at the bank that the clerk had not yet returned from his trip to the town of Russellville, where he had been sent. In that way nothing came out that would spoil Larry's chance for a beat. He got a fine exclusive tale about the finding of the empty valise.

"And now what are you going to do, Larry?" asked Mr. Emberg, when Larry reported at the office of the *Leader*.

"I'm going to get after Witherby," declared the young reporter.

"But how?"

"I don't know yet. He must have left some kind of a trail. I'm going to Russellville, and see what time he left, and what train he took."

"He evidently came back to New York, by all accounts."

"Yes, and I'm going to have my own troubles to trace him from there. New York is so big."

"I'm afraid I've given you too hard an assignment, Larry."

"No, Mr. Emberg. I'll get to the bottom of this mystery yet. You just wait."

But several days went by, and Larry had to admit that he was baffled at every turn. The Russellville clews availed him nothing.

One afternoon he came in from reporting a big fire, to find a telegram awaiting him. Eagerly he tore it open.

"Anything of importance, Larry?" asked the city editor, who was passing through the room at that moment.

"I don't know," answered the reporter, "and yet it might be. It's a wire from Bert Bailey, the old fisherman on the Jersey coast, who figured in the finding of Mr. Potter, the missing millionaire, you remember."

"What does he say?"

"Why, he tells me he has a story for me. I asked him to let me know whenever anything unusual occurred down there, and he wires me this:

"'Queer man down here. Seems to be made of money. Better come down.'"

"Made of money!" cried the city editor. "Larry, get right after that. Get on the trail at once! I believe that is Witherby who is hiding there!"

CHAPTER XX

A LONG CHASE

SEVEN MILE BEACH, on the Jersey coast, was the place where Larry had once had an assignment to cover a story about a wreck of a steamship, and was also his starting point in the hunt for Mr. Potter, the missing millionaire. It was there he had met Bert Bailey, an old fisherman, who had helped him.

And it was toward Seven Mile Beach that Larry now turned his attention. No sooner had he received the telegram than he reached for a timetable of trains that ran to that rather-out-of-the-way coast resort.

"Can you make it this afternoon, Larry?" asked Mr. Emberg.

"Well, there's a train that will bring me there after midnight," answered the young reporter. "I'll take that."

"Hadn't you better wait until to-morrow?" suggested the city editor.

"No indeed!" exclaimed Larry. "I've done enough waiting on this case as it is. I want to get busy. This may be the beginning of the end. If that's Witherby hiding there I'll soon be after him, and, if I don't find the million dollars, I'll get the thief, anyhow, and a corking good story, too."

"Do you think this clew will amount to anything?"

"Well, it's hard to say. Naturally I'm hopeful, and when I hear of a queerly acting man, in a lonely fishing hamlet, who is spending a lot of money, it makes me think it might be Witherby. Of course, it may not be, but I've got to make sure. I'll let you know by wire as soon as anything developes."

In order to lose no time, Larry telephoned to his mother that he had to go out of town, and would not be back for several days perhaps. Then, having sent a boy up to get a few of his clothes in a valise, while Larry himself arranged about buying a ticket to Seven Mile Beach, the young reporter was ready to start.

He had a last talk with the bank president, telling him of the new developments.

"I'm sure I hope something comes of this!" exclaimed Mr. Bentfield. "Things will come to a crisis soon, if we don't find the thief. All our employees are uneasy, from being virtually under suspicion, and I don't know how long I can keep up the innocent, little deception about Witherby being away on business. They will soon suspect that he had fled, and that he is the one who took the million."

"And yet, with all that, he may be innocent," said Larry, "though I don't believe it."

"Certainly he is the only one, in all the bank, on whom such strong suspicion has fallen," declared the president. "And, though the officers are still keeping a careful watch, not one of the other clerks shown any guilty uneasiness, nor has any one of them shown a disposition to go away, unannounced."

"If any one does flee, I had better be notified," suggested Larry. "You can send a telegram in care of Bert Bailey."

It was a long, and not very pleasant, ride to Seven Mile Beach. Most of it had to be made after dark, and Larry dozed fitfully in his seat, half thinking and half dreaming, of the bank mystery on which he had worked so faithfully.

The car was almost deserted, for there was not much travel at this time of night. It was close to twelve o'clock, and Larry knew that he must be near his destination. He dozed off, and awoke suddenly, to hear a dash of rain against the window. Almost at the same moment the train came to a sudden stop.

"Something's wrong!" exclaimed Larry, sitting up. He had traveled enough to know that the application of the air brakes with such force did not mean an ordinary stop. And, peering out into the darkness, as best he could, he could see no sign of a station.

The young reporter was about to go out, and see what was the trouble, when a brakeman came in, and Larry made inquiry of him.

"Something went wrong with the engine," was the answer. "They only give us half-worn out locomotives on this division, anyhow."

"Will we be held up long?"

"Until morning I guess."

"How far are we from Seven Mile Beach?"

"About three miles."

"Then I'm going to walk. I'm in a hurry." Larry made up his mind that the least delay that could be avoided ought to be, if he was to capture the thief. "Witherby may skip any moment, night or day." he reflected.

"Walk! In this rain?" asked the brakeman, as there came a patter of drops against the window. "I wouldn't. I'm going to make myself snug in here. There's nothing we can do, the engineer says, and they can't get another locomotive to us until morning. This division goes to sleep after ten o'clock I guess. Walk, in this rain? I guess not!"

"You would if you were a newspaper reporter," thought Larry grimly, as he reached for his valise in the rack over his head.

It was not a very inviting prospect that lay before him. The night was dark, and the rain came down heavily. The railroad ran along the beach at this point, and Larry knew that by following the strand he would eventually come to his destination, and the little cabin where Bert Bailey lived. Fortunately he had an umbrella, but as he stepped off the train he found that the wind was blowing in from the sea with such violence that it whipped the drops up under the umbrella, making it all but useless.

Larry never forgot that long, dismal walk. When he had passed the locomotive, at which the fireman and engineer, with flickering lanterns, were tinkering, and got beyond the rays of the headlight, it seemed as if he had been plunged into a damp pit of blackness. Off to the left the waves rolled and thundered on the sand, and overhead was the rain, while the wind blew with increasing violence. Larry kept to the railroad track, the walking being better there than on the sand.

"Whew! This is fierce!" he exclaimed, as a gust, stronger than any of the preceding ones, nearly tore the umbrella from his grasp. "This is the worst I've struck in a long time. But I've got to keep on. If Witherby hasn't skipped out yet, this storm may keep him back."

Larry trudged on. He was almost wet through, and he was beginning to feel chilly though it was summer. But he knew that his tramp must soon end and, a little later, he saw the dim outlines of the few houses that composed the little hamlet where Bailey, the fisherman, lived.

"I hope he has a fire, and can give me some hot coffee," mused Larry, as he stumbled on in the darkness. "This place has not changed much since I was here before. I don't see any sky-scrapers," he added, "and the taxicab service seems to be put out of commission by the rain."

He swung away from the track now, and cut across the sands toward the fisherman's cabin. He looked, but could make out no light in it.

"He's gone to bed I guess," thought the reporter. "Well, I'll have to rouse him. I suppose I should have sent him a message saying I was coming, but I didn't have time."

He knocked on the door, and waited. There was no response.

"Jove! I hope he isn't away from home," thought Larry. "I don't know where else I could stay to-night." He looked around on the storm-swept waste of sand, and knocked again. This time a voice called:

"Who's there?"

"Larry Dexter," was the answer. "I came down after I got your telegram, Mr. Bailey. Where's the queer man with the money?"

"Oh, land-lubber's luck!" exclaimed the fisherman, as he struck a light, and opened the door. "Good land, Mr. Dexter! And to think of you coming down all this way in the storm! Oh, Davy Jones! Oh, lee scuppers!"

"Why, what's the matter?" asked Larry, surprised at the fisherman's words and actions. "Is anything wrong?"

"The man's skipped!" exclaimed Bert Bailey.

"Skipped?" cried Larry.

"Yep. Lit out late this afternoon. I sent you a wire after my first one, but I guess you didn't get it. Sit down by the fire, and I'll tell you about it while I make coffee, and get you something to eat. To think of your coming down all this way, and getting fooled. It's too bad!"

The kitchen fire was going, and the fisherman turned on the drafts to brighten it. Soon a pot of coffee was boiling, while Larry got rid of some of his wet garments.

"Now tell me about the man," he urged. "Maybe, after all, he isn't the one I'm after."

"He was a fellow of about your size, and he wore a sandy moustache," said the fisherman. "He had a valise with the letters 'H. W.' on the end, though he gave it out that his name was Thomas Dawson. He walked with a limp."

"Pshaw, then it can't be Witherby!" cried Larry, who had been hopeful when he heard about the sandy moustache. "That is, unless he adopted the limp as a disguise. But go on. Tell me more."

"He came here a few days ago," went on the fisherman, "and hired a small cabin of me. Gave it out that he wanted a rest. But, say, you ought to have seen him spend money!"

"Did he?" cried Larry eagerly, all his old suspicions reviving. "How much. Was it in thousand-dollar bills?"

"No; I couldn't say they was," replied Bert Bailey slowly. "But he sure was lavish. Why, he used to buy five-cent cigars at the store, and everybody around here smokes twofers."

"Twofers?"

"Yes, two for five cents, you know, an' they're expensive enough for anybody. An' then this feller give Hank Solomon half a dollar one day, jest for rowin' him out in the bay after fish. He didn't git none, neither. Why, fifty cents! Hank never gets more than twenty-five. Say, that feller was just made of money!"

Once more Larry's heart sank. Clearly the old fisherman, with exaggerated ideas of the value of money, had brought the reporter down on a wild-goose chase.

"You said in your telegram that he acted strangely," said Larry, to Bert Bailey. "What did you mean?"

"Well, I guess you'd call it queer if you went past his cabin at all hours of the night, and heard him ravin' about a big theft, and the loss of papers, and all such. Sometimes he'd be yellin' for some one to unhand him, whatever that is, and again he'd yell suthin' about he must git them papers. Once I heard him cry out: 'Officer, do your duty!' Now, if that ain't queer I'd like to know what is."

"You heard him say these things?" asked Larry, a new idea coming into his mind.

"Sure I did. He was talkin' in his sleep I reckon, for it was mostly at night I'd hear him. Then, too, he went about as if he didn't know what to do next—sort of lookin' up at the clouds, and talking to himself. Oh, he was queer, all right, and he certainly blew in his money. I remembered you said you'd like to hear when there was any news down here, and so I telegraphed you. I'm sorry, though, you had your trip for nothing, but late this afternoon that feller went off, bag and baggage."

"I don't know that I've had my trip for nothing," said Larry, all excitement once more. "In fact, I'm beginning to believe now that this man is the very one I'm after."

Briefly he told about the theft of the million dollars, and the disappearance of Witherby.

"Whales' teeth and lobsters' tails!" cried the fisherman. "A million dollars! No wonder he bought five-centers! Whew!"

"Do you know where he went?" asked Larry, eagerly.

"No, but maybe you can find out at the depot, in the mornin', where his ticket was to. The place ain't open now. And so you think he's the thief?"

"I'm almost sure of it. He probably came here as the most out-of-the-way place he could find, to be under cover for a day or so. His talk, in his sleep probably, was because he has been continually fearing arrest for the last month. His conscience troubles him. I'll get right after him in the morning."

Larry fell into an uneasy sleep, and as soon as it was daylight he paid a visit to the cabin that the mysterious man had occupied. The reporter hoped to find some sort of a clew, nor was he disappointed.

Among some odds and ends of trash, in a box, were the pieces of a torn envelope. Barry fitted them together, and got the name "Harrison Witherby." The envelope had been addressed to him in Hackenford.

"By Jove!" cried the young reporter in delight. "It *was* Witherby who was here! The trail is still good! Now if I can only find out where he's gone!"

He hurried to the railroad station and made inquiries of the ticket agent. That official remembered the mysterious man very well, for he did not sell many tickets to strangers.

"And where did he go?" asked Larry, with beating heart.

"To Chicago," was the unexpected answer.

"You'll never get him now!" exclaimed Bert Bailey, who went to the depot with the reporter.

"Yes I will!" cried Larry determinedly. "Give me a ticket."

"Where to?" asked the agent.

"To Chicago. I'm going there on the next train!"

CHAPTER XXI
IN THE THEATRE

LARRY wired a brief account of his trip, and the necessity for a change in his plans, to Mr. Emberg, and also to the bank president. Then, having said good-bye to the fisherman, promising to let him know how his long chase ended, the young reporter started for Chicago.

The line running to Seven Mile Beach was a branch of the Pennsylvania Railroad, and it would be over that road that Larry would make his advent into the Windy City. So, also, would Witherby, he reflected.

"Only I'll be several hours behind him," Larry thought, "and I'll have my own troubles locating him. It will be almost as bad as it would have been in New York. But I'll get him!"

Just how he was going to do it Larry did not know. He thought it all over on the long trip to Chicago, but could decide on no plan that satisfied him.

"I suppose I could walk through the streets, looking for Witherby, disguised as he was last," thought the young reporter. "I might come across him, but it would take a good while, unless luck was with me. Then, of course, I could go to the police, but I haven't much information to give them. And, if they got to looking for Witherby, the story would come out in the papers here, and the *Leader* wouldn't get any benefit of it.

"No; I've got to play a lone hand in this game, and see what I can do. Of course, when it comes to the end, and I see Witherby, I'll have to call on an officer to arrest him. Then I can wire the story to New York."

The more Larry thought over the matter, though, the more he became convinced that to go idly about the streets looking for the bank thief was not the best method.

"I've got to have some starting point," he reasoned, "and I guess the railroad depot would be the best place. He will arrive in Chicago over this line, and I can make inquiries in the station if any of the men employed there have seen a chap fixed up like Witherby. Though it's going to be like hunting for a needle in a haystack."

Larry, indeed, found this so when he reached Chicago, and began his inquiries. No one in the big depot, to whom he applied, had seen any one resembling the fugitive.

"Say, young feller," said one of the door-tenders, "there's thousands of people in here every day, and to remember any one he'd have to be the President of the United States, or a man with a blue nose, or something like that."

Larry agreed that this was so, for a person would have to have a distinct personality to be picked out from amid the ever-shifting throngs.

"Well, that clew isn't going to amount to anything," he decided as he went to a quiet hotel, where he intended spending his time while in Chicago. "Now for the next one."

"Let's see. What would be the most natural thing for a fellow, who had run off with a million dollars, to do? Would he go to a big, swell hotel, and begin to spend money like water? Not unless he wanted to be talked about, and raise suspicions. What would he do, then?"

Larry paused a moment in his self cross-examination.

"Why, he'd look for a quiet place," he reasoned. "A place where he wouldn't be much observed. Not too quiet, either, for in a place like that there are not enough people but what some one knows the business affairs of every one else. He'd pick out a small hotel, or a fairly large boarding-house," went on Larry, thinking to himself in the quiet of his hotel room. "Then the thing for me to do is to make a round of these places, and ask about all new arrivals. And I'd better get a letter, or something, from the chief of police here to show I'm not a second-story man, or a gold-brick worker."

Larry easily arranged, after telegraphing to the New York chief of police whom he knew well, to get a letter from the head of the Chicago police, authorizing him to make inquiries. The young reporter did not tell just for whom he was looking, promising, however, that when it came time for an arrest that the Chicago police would be given due notice, and credit. Then Larry began what was to prove a tedious search.

He visited hotel after hotel, and boarding-house after boarding-house. In each one he inquired for a recent arrival, who might be disguised in a variety of ways. He could give a good description of Witherby's characteristics, which the young man would find hard to change, no matter what disguise he adopted.

But the search seemed likely to end in nothing, and the young reporter was beginning to feel discouraged. Still he would not give up. He wrote to Mr. Emberg, to find out if the paper wanted to go to the expense of keeping him in Chicago, on what seemed a useless assignment. He received word back to stick as long as he wanted to, and to rush the story whenever he found Witherby.

Two weeks passed. Larry thought he had covered all the possible small hotels, or boarding-houses, in Chicago, where his man might be likely to stay. But by referring to a list he had made, he found that he still had several days' work ahead of him.

"Well, I'm going to take a night off, anyhow," said the young reporter one evening. "I'm going to the theatre, and forget all about this case. Maybe, if I freshen up, I'll get a new idea to work on."

He picked out, from among several attractions, one he thought would be amusing and bought his ticket. The play was a good one and Larry thoroughly enjoyed it. He had succeeded in forgetting all about the bank mystery, for a time, but, with the final fall of the curtain, the problem came back to him with more force than ever.

As he walked toward his hotel, having cut through a narrow alley on which the stage door of the theatre opened, the young reporter saw several of the performers coming out.

Many of the young women were met by their brothers, or other escorts. Larry looked on curiously, for, though he had been behind the scenes several times, there was always a fascination about the life of an actor or actress.

A little crowd of performers came out together, calling good-nights to each other, and at the sound of one voice Larry started. Where had he heard it before?

A moment later he knew, for, as a young man leaving the shadow of the stage door passed under a glaring arc light, Larry saw the features of Harrison Witherby!

And the bank clerk wore no false beard or moustache. In fact, aside from a rather "loud" suit of clothes, he was dressed ordinarily.

For a moment Larry could not believe his eyesight, but after a second glance, he knew he could not be mistaken.

"It is Witherby!" he whispered to himself. "I've found him! He must be paying attention to some actress! That's why he's been back of the scenes. But—he's all alone. I don't understand that." For Witherby had moved off down the street, a solitary figure.

"I've got to follow him!" thought Larry desperately. "I've got to keep right after him until I find where he's staying. Then I'll have him arrested. To think that I've found him, after all! I wonder where he has that million dollars? I wonder, if he went back of the scenes, to escort some actress home, why she isn't with him?"

Then Larry realized that Witherby might have gone in merely to pay a congratulatory call, or there might have been some misunderstanding.

"He seemed to know several of the performers," reasoned the reporter, "for he said 'good-night' to two or three of them. What can he be doing, getting so thick with theatrical people? Well, I'll find that out later. Just now I've got to follow him, and I mustn't let him see me!"

Then Larry started to trail the suspected bank clerk, who sauntered down the street, jauntily swinging a cane.

CHAPTER XXII

THE ARREST

WHILE it was easy for Larry to follow Witherby along the streets, which, at that hour of the night, were not crowded, it was not so easy to avoid observation because of that same absence of people. And Larry certainly did not want the former bank clerk to suspect him.

"For if he does, he'll know right away what's up, and he'll disappear with the million, and I'll have all my work to do over again. I certainly was lucky to spot him this time, and lucky lightning would never strike twice again like this. I've got to keep out of sight."

It was only by cleverly dodging behind tree boxes, and house-stoops that the reporter was able to remain unobserved. Several times Witherby turned sharply, as though he suspected he was being followed, but Larry was too quick for him.

"My, he lives a good way from the theatre," thought Larry, as he followed along, block after block. "I wish I knew what he was doing there. If I knew which of the performers he cared about, I might be able to get a line on him that way. Guess I'll make some inquiries. It may be—"

Larry had no time to finish his sentence, for Witherby turned suddenly, and, as Larry was just then under a street lamp, he had to dodge quickly behind the post.

"I wonder if he saw me?" mused the reporter. "He is certainly suspicious."

But this proved to be the end of the chase, for, a moment later, Witherby went up the steps of a house which bore the sign "*BOARDING*" in a window. Larry made a mental note of the street and number, and also looked at the surroundings.

The street was a quiet one, with a number of apartment houses of the poorer class on either side. The house that Witherby had entered was near a corner, and this cross street was traversed by a trolley line. The neighborhood seemed to be an old-fashioned part of the city.

"Well I've found his stopping-place," thought Larry, "and the next thing is to settle how he's to be arrested. I can't go in there, and get him single-handed, and I haven't a warrant on which the police could take him. Nor could a policeman go in there and get him to-night. In the excitement he might get away with the million, if he had it hidden in his room, as is likely the case.

"And yet he must be arrested. But how? I think he's safe enough until morning, and by then I'll think of a plan. I hate to leave this neighborhood, but I've got to."

Larry was in a quandary. Though he was morally certain that Witherby was the thief, all the evidence against him, so far, was circumstantial. It might not be wise to arrest him on suspicion, for, if the charge should fail, then Witherby could sue Larry, the bank, and the paper for false arrest.

"And we don't want that to happen," thought the young reporter. "It would be bad all around. If I could only get him arrested on some trivial charge which would hold him until Mr. Bentfield or some bank official could get here, that would answer. Then they could take the responsibility.

"By Jove, I have it. I'll pay him back for what he did to Miss Mason in the subway. I'll come back here to-morrow, and wait for him to come out of that boarding-house. Then I'll walk past, and pretend that he collided with me. I'll accuse him of doing it on purpose. I'll get into a fight with him if necessary, and raise such a row that the police will come. Then I'll make a charge of assault and battery against him. That will be sufficient on which to hold him. I'll wire Mr. Bentfield right away, to come to Chicago on the first train."

Now that he had formed a plan of action Larry felt better satisfied. He hurried to his hotel, and that morning he began his vigil at the boarding-house. He reasoned that Witherby might come out at any time, and he wanted to be ready for him.

He had not been waiting more than an hour before a quick glance up the street, from the corner where he had been standing, as though waiting for a car, showed him the man he wanted coming down the steps.

Witherby was standing with his back toward our hero, and so did not see him at first. Larry, hurrying up, reached the foot of the steps just as the bank clerk came down them. By cleverly lurching forward, Larry managed to make it seem as if Witherby had collided with him. The force of the impact was more than Larry had counted on, and Witherby went down with an exclamation of anger.

Larry decided to act at once. Before the bank clerk could get up the reporter seized him by the collar, exclaiming:

"What do you mean by running into me? I believe you tried to pick my pocket! I shall have you arrested!"

Larry assumed a virtuous indignation. Witherby, taken quickly by surprise, glanced up, and a look of amazement came over his face at the sight of Larry. The bank clerk had on no disguise, unless a "loud" checked suit, and a polka-dot velvet vest, of the kind sometimes worn by theatrical men, could be so called. His hat had rolled some distance away on the sidewalk.

"What! You here, Dexter?" cried Witherby. "What does this mean? Let go of me! Let go of me at once!"

But Larry had no such intention. A glance down the street showed him an officer approaching, and, still keeping hold of Witherby's collar with one hand, with the other Larry beckoned for the club-swinging policeman to hasten.

The officer ran up, exclaiming:

"What's the row? What's the trouble here?"

"Nothing!" exclaimed Witherby. "What do you mean by this, Dexter?"

"I make a charge of assault and battery against this fellow," said Larry boldly. "He tried to pick my pocket, I think."

"I did not!" cried Witherby. "It's all a mistake!"

"Well, I'll take you both down to the station house, and you can explain to the captain," spoke the officer, and a little later, when the patrol wagon came, Larry and his captive were put into it. This was just what the young reporter wanted, but Witherby was very angry.

"There is something back of this!" cried the former bank clerk, when Larry had told of the collision. "You're not having me arrested for colliding with you, Dexter. What is it?"

"You're wanted for robbing the Consolidated Bank of one million dollars!" said Larry quietly, "and President Bentfield will soon be here to press the charge. I ask that he be held until then," he said to the police captain.

"A million dollars!" gasped the police official. "You don't mean to say this is the fellow who is responsible for that big Wall Street bank mystery?"

Larry nodded.

"Say!" cried Witherby, after an open-mouthed stare at Larry. "You're away off! A million dollars! Why, I had no more to do with the taking of that than you did. I can explain everything if you'll give me a chance."

"You'll have all the chance you want," declared Larry. "I've got plenty of evidence against you. I saw the thousand-dollar bill in your room. I saw you trying on a black beard, I found a sandy moustache in your room. The bricks that were in the dummy bag came from a new house right back of you in Hackenford. I traced you to Seven Mile Beach. I traced you here. You had the million all right. You bought the duplicate valise of Miss Mason, and I found where you hid it behind the old ledgers, the one that held the money. I've got you right!"

"Say, either you're crazy, or I am!" exclaimed Witherby simply, when Larry had finished. "I don't know any more about that million than you do, though I can see why and how you suspected me. I did have a thousand-dollar bill, and I did disguise myself in a false beard and moustache. But I never knew any of the bricks were near me. I can explain everything."

"How?" asked Larry incredulously.

"In the shortest way, by saying that I have become an actor, and that the false beard and moustache are part of my outfit. I practiced wearing them back in Hackenford to get used to them, and I wore them publicly to see if people could detect them. I wanted to get a perfect make-up for the part I'm playing here."

"You an actor?" gasped Larry, now all at sea. "So that's why you were in the theatre?"

"Exactly, and you've made a fine mess of it," sneered the former bank clerk. "Though, I admit, perhaps my actions were suspicious. But I can explain everything."

"About the thousand-dollar bill, and leaving town so suddenly?" asked Larry.

"Yes. That bill was given me by Mr. Wilson, one of the bank directors. He befriended me when no one else would, and he got me my place in the bank. I always wanted to be an actor, and I only worked in the Consolidated until I had a chance to get on the stage. I was always rehearsing in private. Mr. Wilson heard of my ambition, and, as his father was a celebrated actor, he had sympathy for me and he gave me a thousand dollars to start my career. That's where the money came from. I didn't want to take the money at first, and thought I might return it. That's why I didn't bank it or change the bill."

"But why did you leave so suddenly?"

"Because, most unexpectedly, I got the very chance for which I was waiting. A member of the company playing here left suddenly. The manager wired for me to come on to Chicago in a few days. It was the same day Mr. Bentfield sent me out of town, and I did not want to go. But I went, and I finished up the business for him. Then I hurried back to my boarding-house, got the thousand dollars and my things, and left. I went away disguised, as I did not want to stop and explain why I was leaving, and I did not want to be arrested and detained as a suspect. I heard about that quiet cabin at Seven Mile Beach, and I went there to rest up and get letter-perfect in my actor part. What you say Bailey heard, about me raving, was probably when I was going over my part."

"But, why didn't you send some word to the bank about leaving?" asked Larry, after a moment's thought.

"Because I knew any explanation I might make would be construed as an excuse for getting away to avoid suspicion of the theft. I was afraid they would suspect me if I left, and I was right. I know several of the clerks who want to leave the bank, but they are afraid to, for fear they'll be arrested. I took the first and best chance that came. I didn't even tell Mr. Wilson that I was going until I was away. But, as for that million dollars, I never had a penny of it!"

"Then who took it?" asked Larry weakly. He saw his case, that he had built up with such care, tumbling apart. He did not know what to do next. And yet he was rather glad on the whole, for the sake of Grace Potter, that Witherby was not the thief.

"I didn't!" declared Witherby, "though I can see now that my use of beards and moustaches led to that belief."

"Indeed it did," declared Larry, remembering the time he had seen the clerk in the costumer's at the time of the drug house fire. "I'm sorry I knocked you down, and caused your arrest. I admit I was suspicious of you ever since that—er—well, that little fracas in the subway."

"I'm sorry about that," admitted Witherby. "I was in a hurry that morning, and late. Besides I had a terrible toothache, and I didn't care much what I did. I wish you'd apologize to that young lady for me."

"I will," agreed Larry, who was beginning to have a different feeling toward Witherby. "She thought sure, from a back view of you in the store one day, that you were the bearded man who had bought the duplicate bag."

"Well, I didn't. Though I hurried out, as I didn't want to meet you. I'm going to write to Mr. Bentfield and Mr. Wilson at once, explaining everything. I realize that I came away rather unceremoniously, and under suspicious circumstances. But if I had given the usual notice, and waited two weeks before leaving, I would have missed the chance to get on the stage. And I may say that I have started on a successful stage career."

"I'm glad to hear it," spoke Larry. "But I certainly am puzzled. I'll have to begin all over again, and I don't know how to do it."

"Then I suppose there is no charge to be made?" suggested the police captain.

"None," answered Larry, "unless Mr. Witherby wants to get even with me."

"I'm satisfied to let the matter drop," was the answer. "I ought to be at the theatre now for rehearsal. And to think you have been trailing me, thinking I had the million dollars!"

"Yes, I made a big mistake," admitted Larry. "But I'll get the real thief yet, and find the money."

"I hope you do," spoke Witherby. "Come and see me act to-night."

"I saw you last night, but I didn't recognize you," said Larry, with a smile.

"I took the part of the old servant," explained the actor, and then the reporter recognized the character as one of the principal ones in the play. Witherby had acted well.

"I guess this case is closed so far as we are concerned then," spoke the police captain, and, taking the hint Larry and Witherby went out. Each had a new respect for the other.

"What are you going to do next?" asked the actor.

"I don't know," replied Larry. "Get to New York as fast as I can, for one thing, and then look for new clews."

He was quite despondent as he went back to his hotel, while Witherby kept on to rehearsal.

"Telegram for you," said the hotel clerk, as Larry entered the lobby. He took it, wondering what it might contain.

CHAPTER XXIII
ON A NEW TRACK

WITH a quick motion Larry ripped the end off the envelope. A glance gave him the contents of the message. It was from his city editor, Mr. Ember, and read:

"Come back at once. Another bank clerk has skipped. He may be the real one."

"Another clerk disappeared!" exclaimed Larry. "Say, this is getting to be worse than the fifteen puzzle. First Witherby drops out of sight, and, after a long chase, I find him, but he isn't the one wanted. And I believe he told the truth, for everything he said fitted in. Now here's another one gone. I wonder who he is, and what it means?"

But Larry knew he had no time for idle speculation. He hurriedly packed his valise, and caught the first train he could for New York. Before he left, however, he received a visit from the theatrical manager who had engaged Witherby. The manager confirmed all that the former bank clerk had said.

On his way to the metropolis Larry thought of many things. Among them was the possibility that, after all, Witherby might be the guilty one, in spite of what the manager had said.

"But what could I do?" asked Larry. "I had no proof, and I could not have him held. He could have walked out of the police station, as far as the theft charge was concerned. And by Jove! I've wired for Mr. Bentfield to come on to Chicago! I wonder if I can stop him from making a useless trip?"

It was a slim chance, but Larry took it. At the first place his train stopped he sent a message to the bank president, apprising him of the change in the situation, and telling him not to come on west. Fortunately, Mr. Bentfield had not started yet, in response to Larry's first telegram, so the second one caught him, and he remained in New York.

"Well, who is missing now?" asked Larry, of the bank president on his arrival in the metropolis, after his trip from Chicago.

"One whom we least suspected," replied the president. "One of our oldest and most trusted clerks, one who led a highly moral life, and was well up in church work. It is a great shock to all of us, for there is little doubt now but that he is the thief."

"We thought Witherby was," spoke Larry, with a smile, "but we were mistaken."

"There can be no doubt in this case," went on the bank president.

"Why not?"

"Because he left a note, confessing to the theft, before he went away."

"Left a note!" cried Larry. "Where is it? Has the story come out? Did the *Leader* get it?"

"No, but you will soon have it. I arranged with Mr. Emberg, in consideration of what you have done for us, to keep the matter of this clerk's disappearance quiet, until you returned. You are to have the exclusive story, and—"

"And then I'm going to get on this new trail!" cried Larry. "I made a fizzle of the other one, but I won't in this case. Where is the note? Who is the confessed thief?"

"Harry Norton, our chief clerk," was the sorrowful answer of the president. "I would have trusted him as I would my own son, but the temptation was too much for him. Here is the note I found on my desk the other morning. That day Norton did not appear for work, and he has disappeared."

He handed over a single sheet of paper. Larry read:

"Please have suspicions removed from all others. I alone am guilty. I took the million dollars, and hid the empty valise. I am going far away, so there is no use of pursuing me. I have the million—what is left of it—with me. I write this, so that no one else may be unjustly suspected, as I fear is now the case."

It was signed with Norton's name.

"What do you think of that?" asked the bank president.

"Well, it looks genuine," admitted Larry, "especially as you say he has disappeared. But I am not so sure about what he says here, that pursuit is useless."

"Do you think there is a hope of catching him?" asked the president eagerly.

"I'm going to make a big try," replied Larry. "We have several things in our favor. I'm going to get right on this case, but first the story must go to my paper."

"Certainly," agreed Mr. Bentfield, and Larry hurried in, to write what proved to be another big "beat" in the bank mystery case. All the other papers were scooped.

"And now to get after Mr. Norton!" exclaimed Larry to his city editor, as the young reporter closed his desk on his typewriter.

"Have you any plan, Larry?"

"Not much of one. In the first place, I'm going out to Norton's house, and see what I can learn. I want to get there before the other reporters overrun the place."

Harry Norton lived in a modest, though well-built, house on Staten Island. He was a bachelor, and an aged sister kept house for him. As Larry was on his way to the home of the missing clerk, he went over the details of the robbery. He realized that Norton, as well as Witherby, had been in a position to take the valise filled with money, and substitute another filled with bricks for it. Though just how the exchange was made was not yet clear to him.

The first thing Larry noticed, on reaching the house, was a little pile of bricks in a side yard. He knew them at once as the same kind that had been in the valise. They were some left, of a quantity that had been used to repair a fireplace in the clerk's home, he learned later.

"So here is where Norton got them," he reasoned. "He could pick them up at his leisure, and no one would be any the wiser. He could bring them to the bank in a valise any time. So far so good!"

Larry found the aged sister in tears, for already she had heard of her brother's disgrace. At first she would have nothing to say to the young reporter, but he finally prevailed on her to talk.

She could say little of consequence, however, and Larry was sure she knew nothing of her brother's whereabouts.

On his way out of the house the young reporter saw something lying on a hall table. He picked it up, shoved it quickly into his pocket, and hurried away.

"I rather think, unless I get fooled again, that this will help me find the man with the million," mused Larry.

As he passed down a side street he saw Peter Manton, his rival, going up to the house.

"Too late again!" said Larry to himself, with a smile.

CHAPTER XXIV

IN PURSUIT

EVERY paper in New York was fairly bristling with the new development in the million-dollar bank mystery. All the stories concerned the note of confession left by Norton, his flight, and the possibility of catching him, and getting back the million.

Of course, the *Leader* had the story first, but it did not go into such "spasms" as did the other sheets. In fact, after the first account written by Larry, little was printed on the case.

Not so the other journals. They went into the life history of the absconding clerk, from the time when he was a little boy up to the present, and some even had pictures supposed to be his, taken when an infant.

Of course, pictures of him as he looked just before making his escape were scattered broadcast. They were even on the police circulars, offering the twenty thousand dollars reward, and good likenesses they were.

The police of the entire country, private and public detectives—in fact, the minions of the law of two continents—were on the alert to capture Norton, for the big reward was attractive bait. And yet, after three days had passed since he had left the note of confession, no trace of him was found.

The police had gone over every clew with a fine-tooth comb, but had found nothing. All the missing man's associates at the bank knew that he had been among them one day, no more suspected that any one was. The next day he did not come to work. Then the note was found.

All his sister knew was that he had come home as usual one afternoon, had gone to bed early, and the next morning he was not in his room, nor had his bed been slept in. He had disappeared as silently and mysteriously as if the earth had opened and swallowed him, and the million dollars was apparently with him.

"And you expect, after all these others have failed, to find him; do you, Larry?" asked Mr. Emberg, as the young reporter and the city editor were talking over the case. It was a few days after Larry's return from his visit to the home of the missing clerk.

"I'm going to find him," declared Larry, "that is, if you consent to my plan, and furnish me with the auto."

"Oh, you can have the auto all right, but I don't quite see how you are going to make good in it. What makes you hold to your theory?"

"Because of this." Larry held up the object he had secured on his visit to the clerk's home. It was nothing but an automobile catalogue, but, on looking through it, Larry had found a page turned down at an illustration showing a powerful car. And on the margin of that page were the penciled words: 'This one!'

"Then you think—?" began the city editor.

"I'm almost sure that Norton bought an automobile, and that he is on his way to some place of hiding in it. In fact, I know that the car was delivered to him here in New York, and that he started off in it."

"You do? Then why haven't you started after him?"

"Because I only learned that a little while ago. I was puzzling my brains over how to get on his trail, and I never thought of the perfectly simple plan of going to the headquarters of the automobile concern here. As soon as I thought of that I went there, and they told me they had sold a man of Norton's description a powerful car. He drove off at once in it. He had a valise with him. Probably that contained the million."

"But look here, Larry. A man can't go in a place, buy an auto, and start off with it as if it was a baby carriage," objected the city editor. "He has to know how to run a car, you know, and he has to have a license, and all that sort of thing. It isn't so simple as it sounds."

"It was in Norton's case. He lives in Staten Island. He has had a small runabout car for about a year, and knows how to run it. He has a New York license, and not long ago he had his new car registered, and so all he had to do was to go to the place, get in it, and start off."

"Then why hasn't he been arrested before this, Larry? He is a big man, and one easily picked out of a crowd. His picture has been scattered broadcast. Why hasn't he been arrested?"

"For the simple reason that he left his car in his garage—I mean, the little runabout. I believe no one suspects that he has a new and powerful one. He bought it under an assumed name. Then, too, with a cap on, an auto duster, big gloves and goggles, he has the best disguise in the world, and a perfectly natural one. His best friend wouldn't know him."

"Then how are you going to arrest him?"

"I have the number of his car."

"He may change it."

"I don't believe he'd risk that."

"But you don't know where to look for him."

"I think I do," replied Larry confidently. "I believe there is but one place where he would head for with the stolen million in his possession, and that is Canada. For, though it is easier to extradite absconders from there than it used to be, still it is the safest place he could go to, within a short distance of New York. So, if you'll furnish the auto, I'll take after him, and I'll follow on the shortest and best roads that lead to Canada."

"Larry, I believe you're right!" cried Mr. Emberg. "Start as soon as you can, and there's no limit to your expense account. Only get a scoop story if you can."

"I will!" and with that the young reporter began his arrangements.

Two hours later he was driving alone in a powerful car out of New York.

Larry was an expert autoist, and had driven several makes of machines. He held a New York State license, so there was no delay.

After thinking the matter over and consulting a map, Larry picked out what he thought would be the road Norton would most naturally take.

"But he may have switched off, he may have doubled on his trail, and have done any of half a dozen things to baffle pursuit," reasoned Larry, as he skimmed over the road in the powerful car. "So I've got to make inquiries as I go along."

He followed this plan, stopping at road houses and hotels along the way. His task was not the easiest in the world, for the trail was several days old, and autoists were so numerous at this time of the year, that it was difficult for proprietors of hostelries to recall any certain one. But the young reporter was persistent, and by his tact and skill he learned more than an untrained questioner could have done.

But, with all this, he had been traveling for two days before he got his first clew. A man who had charge of autos, whose owners stopped at a certain inn, remembered the powerful car Larry described.

"It was here two days ago," said the attendant.

"Then I've gained one day on him," thought Larry, "for he had three days' start of me. I guess his car isn't as fast as it's supposed to be, or else he isn't getting all out of it that he might. I'll get him yet."

And so the pursuit was kept up. Larry was up early, and he drove until late, taking only short periods of sleep in the hotels along the road. He made constant inquiries, meeting with many disappointments, but occasionally hearing of the man on whose trail he held himself relentlessly. Hour by hour Larry cut down the distance between them.

"I'm gaining! I'm gaining!" he cried in delight when, early one morning, after a stop at a road-house he learned that Norton was but a few hours ahead.

But the Canadian line was nearing rapidly. But for the fact that Norton had taken a roundabout way he would have reached it much sooner. But evidently he believed that he had baffled pursuit, and was taking his time.

"I'm going to catch him to-day!" declared Larry, as he speeded up his car. "Another night, and it will be too late."

Back in New York all the papers save the *Leader* were printing columns about the flight of the clerk, and speculating as to when he would be arrested. In fact, he was "arrested" time and time again, only it proved to be the wrong man. But the young reporter bothered himself not at all about this. He knew he was after his man, and would get him soon unless—

"There's always the possibility of an accident," mused Larry.

Occasionally he wired briefly to Mr. Emberg, but there was no story to print yet, and Larry was holding back for his big beat. The other papers wondered at the strange policy of the *Leader*. All Mr. Emberg used of the bank mystery was an occasional note, when some false arrest was made.

"Larry has something up his sleeve," declared Peter Manton to some other reporters. "He'll beat us yet."

"Nonsense!" exclaimed a veteran correspondent. "We'll beat the *Leader*!"

But Peter shook his head dubiously.

Meanwhile Larry was hot on the trail. That afternoon on stopping to replenish his supply of gasoline he learned with delight that Norton had done the same thing not half an hour before.

"Here's the end of the chase!" exulted Larry, and, jumping into his car he shot ahead, totally disregarding the speed laws.

"And I'm glad for the sake of Grace Potter that it's some one else besides her relative whom I'm after," he murmured.

Five miles farther on, coasting down a hill on a lonely stretch of road, not far from the Canadian line, Larry saw a big car ahead of him. Steering with one hand, Larry focused a pair of opera-glasses on the dangling back number of the machine in front.

"That's him!" cried the young reporter. "Now for the million dollars!"

He pressed the accelerator pedal, and his machine shot ahead like a bolt from a catapult. In a cloud of dust he passed the other vehicle in which a man rode alone. Larry did not give him a backward glance, but, when the young reporter's car was far enough ahead, it came to an abrupt stop. Then Larry backed it squarely across the rather narrow road.

With a screech of the brakes the other man brought his machine to a stop, just in time to avoid a collision.

"What do you mean?" he snarled at Larry. "Are you crazy? Have you had an accident? What are you blocking the road for?"

"So you can't get past," replied Larry calmly.

"So I can't get past? What do you want to stop me for?"

"To get the million dollars belonging to the Consolidated Bank," was the answer.

CHAPTER XXV
THE MILLION DOLLARS

HAD Larry exploded a bombshell under the other man's car, the effect on him would not have been any more startling. And yet, aside from the number of the car, the young reporter had no way of being sure that the man in it was the absconder. Indeed, when he looked at the shrunken frame of the driver, and noted as well as he could behind the goggles the unshaven, haggard face, it was not a bit like Norton's. Yet Larry was sure he was right.

Indeed the man's action on hearing the fateful words was proof enough. He seemed to shrink down in his seat. His hands dropped from the steering-wheel. He gazed blankly at Larry through the big goggles.

"The—the million dollars," he faltered.

"The million dollars, Mr. Norton," said Larry calmly. "I'm from the *Leader*, and I've been following you several days."

"The million dollars," whispered Norton huskily. "The million dollars —yes—yes—"

With a hand that trembled he reached for the spark and gasoline levers, and closed them. The car which had been throbbing and trembling, for it was running free with the clutch out, after the stop became silent. Larry had also shut off his power.

"Well?" asked Larry significantly.

"I—er—I—" began the man, his voice shaking.

"Wait!" cried Larry sternly. "Don't say you haven't got it. It's in the valise you carry. I know the whole story! I've been on this case from the beginning. I followed Witherby to Chicago, and found that he was innocent. I know you are guilty. You have the million. I want it—for the bank, and I'm going to get it!"

Larry's voice rang out clearly.

"Mr. Norton, you may be a desperate man, but I'm desperate, too. I'm going to get it, too. I'll meet force with force!"

There could be but one meaning to that. Norton glanced apprehensively at Larry. The young reporter had one hand in his coat pocket. For an instant the absconder had a wild thought of fight or flight. And then his nerve failed him, and he wilted.

He had made a hard journey, without proper food or sleep, and he was all but exhausted. Larry, though having had a hard time, was still fresh and vigorous. He faced the man relentlessly. Norton quailed before the clear eyes of the young reporter.

"I—" he began again. Larry took a step toward him.

"There is the million!" the absconder suddenly exclaimed, and, tossing aside a lap-robe, he disclosed a valise strapped to the seat beside him. "Take it!" he cried. "I'm glad you found me. Now maybe I'll get some sleep!" and leaning his head on the steering-wheel, he sobbed bitterly.

It was some minutes before Larry knew what to do, for he was much affected. Then he said gently:

"Mr. Norton, you had better come back with me. If you flee it will only make it worse for you, and you will be caught in the end. Will you come?"

"Yes," was the muffled answer. "This is the end. I'm all in!"

Larry reached for the valise, and opened it.

"The money's all there, except a few thousands that I spent," said Norton. "I can pay those back by selling my house. Oh, what a life I've led these last few weeks! What a life!"

It needed but a glance to show Larry that the million was almost intact. Only one of the original packages of thousand-dollar bills had been opened, and that was not much depleted.

"We'll go back in my car," suggested Larry gently. "I think it is in better condition than yours, and we can send for yours later."

Indeed, Norton had driven his car relentlessly and carelessly, and it was much damaged.

Larry stowed the valise carefully in his auto, and then having placed Norton's car to one side of the road, the journey back to the nearest town was begun. The two did not talk much on the trip. Norton sat with bowed head, and occasionally tears fell from his eyes. Larry was genuinely sorry for him, though he knew that punishment must follow, even though the money was recovered.

"I'm afraid—it seems a harsh thing to do—but I'm afraid I shall have to give you into custody," said Larry gently, as they reached the outskirts of the New York town.

"Yes," was the quiet answer. "I sha'n't resist. I—I think perhaps to-night I may get some sleep, even though in a police cell. You—you don't know what it is to lie awake—night after night—listening for some one to come and—and arrest you," he faltered.

Poor, weak Norton was taken to the town jail, and, out of his own pocket, Larry arranged for better care of the prisoner than would ordinarily have been given. For Norton did not retain one cent for himself. He insisted on emptying his pockets into the valise containing most of the million.

"It all belongs to the bank," he said simply. "I'll make up the rest."

"I'm sorry that I have to write unpleasant things about you," said Larry, as he thought of the necessity of getting a story to the *Leader*. "But it is my duty."

"I know," answered the absconder simply. "I'll tell you all that you don't know, which isn't much, I guess," and he smiled sadly. "I'll tell you how I got the money."

Which he did. It was very simple. For a long time he had noticed that large sums were often put in the bank's valise, to be taken by messengers to various financial institutions in New York. This valise, after being filled and locked, would be set down near the cashier's desk, until the messengers called for it, or until the Consolidated men were ready to take it away.

It was from this that Norton got the idea that he could take this bag unobserved, and substitute for it another just like it, but containing bricks instead of bills. He resolved to take a large sum instead of a comparatively small one, and bided his time.

Though he had lived a quiet life up to the time of his temptation, he had in the past few months lost much in speculation, and he needed a large sum to meet his debts. So he decided to take the million.

The first thing needed was a valise exactly like the one used by the bank. Norton got off one day, put on a false beard, and bought the valise of Miss Mason.

The fact that he and Witherby looked alike from the back had deceived the young lady.

Once he had the duplicate valise, Norton filled it with bricks from some left by a mason who made repairs at his house. No one saw him take them, as he wrapped them up after dark.

On the day before the million was to be taken from the Consolidated to the other bank, Norton came to work in the morning carrying the duplicate valise As the clerks often came to the bank, thus equipped to go off on a week-end trip, nothing was thought of Norton's act.

He put his valise—filled with bricks and newspapers as it was—in a small cupboard under his desk, which was a portion of the long, high one in the rear of the grilled cage.

Previously Norton had taken two of the old ledgers from the vault, and had cut off their leather backs. He also had a bottle of liquid glue in readiness.

The million dollars was placed in the mesh-lined bag, and set down on the floor near the chief cashier's desk. It was now time for Norton to act. Watching his chance, he quickly "switched," or transferred, the bags. The one containing the million he placed in his cupboard, and his own, with the bricks in, he placed beside the cashier's desk. Then he closed the cupboard door, and went on with his work. No one had noticed his act. This seems incredible, but almost exactly the same thing was done in a big bank robbery in New York City not many years ago, and the newspapers of November, 1904, tell all about it.

Norton explained to Larry that the exchange was made in about five seconds, and at the time most of the other clerks, or cashiers, in the cage had their backs toward him. What followed is well known.

The messengers departed with the false bag, and the robbery was discovered. But no one knew who had taken the money, nor where it was. No one dreamed that it was in the cupboard, under the desk at which Norton was so innocently working.

Watching his chance, the absconder slipped into the vault with the bag containing the million. Unobserved he pulled out the two ledgers, smeared some liquid glue on their backs, and stuck the backs on the narrow end of the valise. The valise, with the money, he slipped into the space occupied by the books, the ledger backs being outward. It fitted perfectly, and no one looking at the row of old ledgers in the vault would have suspected that two of them consisted of backs only. They were just then, however, worth half a million each. The bulky pages of the ledgers, and the side covers, Norton hid under a pile of dusty, old books.

He now had the million safely hidden away, and it was an easy matter for him, each day, to slip into the vault, and take out a bundle or two of bills. For he had access to the vaults, often having to consult the books there. He always took care to go in alone. In this way, in about a week, he had removed the million, leaving the valise where Larry found it.

And so he got the money, and no one suspected him, for he had a good reputation, and he remained at his work in the bank, though how much nerve it took only he knew.

The rest of the story, how Larry followed the wrong man, though the one to whom suspicion pointed, has been told.

"And now I'm ready to take my medicine," finished Norton. "I thought, after deciding it was time for me to escape, that I could get away. But you caught me. Go, send in your story, Mr. Dexter."

Which Larry did, by long distance 'phone. It was too late for the regular edition of the *Leader*, but Mr. Emberg ordered an extra, and thus Larry secured one of the biggest scoops of his life. For the story was a "beat," and Peter Manton, when the extra came out, said:

"I told you so. I knew Larry would pull it off!"

"Extra! Extra!" yelled the newsboys, with copies of the *Leader* under their arms, as they raced about the City Hall, and along Park Row. "Extra! Full account of the million-dollar robbery! Robber caught! Million found! Reporter solves de big bank mystery!"

There is little more to tell. After telephoning in his story Larry deposited the money in the town bank, and started for New York. He bade Norton good-bye—and a sad farewell it was, but the clerk looked better than he had when Larry stopped him so suddenly on the road.

"I couldn't have kept my secret much longer," he confessed. "All the while I was working in the bank I never knew at what moment suspicion would fall on me. I'm glad it's over."

And Larry was, too, for he had worked hard. The million was soon taken back to the Consolidated Bank, and Norton was given a trial. He received a comparatively light sentence, in consideration of pleading guilty, and of returning the million, for he deeded his house to the bank. I am glad to be able to say that, years afterward, he came from prison a changed man, and until his death led an upright life.

"Well, Larry, I suppose you'll give up reporting now," said his mother, several days after the big case had ended. "You certainly don't need to work so hard, after getting that big reward."

"Oh, I can't give up the newspaper business, mother," he replied. "The ten thousand dollars is a nice sum, but I didn't work up the case for that. I did it for the story and the 'beat.'"

For Larry had refused to accept the full reward, but he took half, and donated the rest to a hospital recently founded by the doctor who had cured Lucy of her spinal trouble.

"Quit the newspaper game? I guess not!" cried Mr. Emberg, when Larry told him of Mrs. Dexter's wish. "We need you on the *Leader*, Larry. I'll save the next big assignment for you."

And what that assignment was, and how Larry "covered" it, may be learned by reading the next book of this series, to be called "Larry Dexter and the Stolen Boy; or, A Chase on the Great Lakes."

"Mr. Dexter, I congratulate you," said Director Wilson to Larry one day. "I admit I didn't take much stock in you at first, but you have won me over. It was a great piece of work. And to think you thought my protégé, Witherby, was the thief!"

"Well, even he admitted that I had a good case against him," said Larry. "By the way, how is he coming on?"

"Splendidly! He is going to be a great actor some day. I am glad I helped him, though I don't say he did just right in leaving the bank so suddenly."

Larry thought the same thing, and as he recalled the various steps he had taken in solving the bank mystery he had no regrets, for he knew that he had acted for the best, and had followed only natural clews. And now, for a time, we will take leave of the young reporter.